The Geek's Dating Coach

Michael Gordon

Published by MG Books, 2024.

This is a work of fiction. Similarities to real people, places, or events are entirely coincidental.

THE GEEK'S DATING COACH

First edition. December 22, 2024.

ISBN: 979-8227200846

Written by Michael Gordon.

Table of Contents

Chapter 1

I sat at the cozy booth in Los Amigos, a vibrant Mexican restaurant in the heart of Virginia Beach, eagerly awaiting my date. The warm ambiance, with its colorful walls adorned with vibrant Mexican artwork and the soft glow of candlelit tables, immediately put me at ease. As a self-proclaimed nerd, I often felt more comfortable in the virtual world of my software development job than in social settings, but there was something about this place that made me feel right at home. The mouth-watering aroma of sizzling fajitas and freshly made tortillas filled the air, tantalizing my taste buds. I mindlessly munched on the crispy tortilla chips, dipping them in the spicy salsa, a perfect combination of tangy and hot flavors. This was my favorite spot in the city, and I couldn't think of a better place to meet someone for the first time.

My name is Cameron Briggs, a 29-year-old software developer with a passion for all things tech and nerdy. My lanky frame was often hunched over a computer screen, coding away, and my thick-rimmed glasses accentuated my serious expression. I was an only child, a bit of a loner, and my social skills were not my forte. High school had been a blur of solitude, with my love for comic books and fantasy movies keeping me company. But now, as a successful entrepreneur, having made my millions in the tech industry, I yearned for a different kind of connection. I wanted to find someone to share my life with, to explore the world beyond my computer screens, and maybe even start a family.

As I waited, my mind drifted to the woman I was about to meet. We had connected online, and after a few promising messages back and forth, we decided to take the plunge and meet in person. I checked my phone for the millionth time, ensuring I hadn't missed any updates, but there was still no sign of her. The chips crunched loudly in my hand, a stark contrast to the soft Latin music playing in the background.

Just as I was about to give up hope, a bubbly voice startled me. "Sorry to interrupt your chip feast, but are you ready to order your entrée, or should I just bring you a basket of those?" I looked up to see a stunning woman with a bright smile and a curvy figure, her dark brown eyes sparkling with mischief. She wore the black uniform of the restaurant, a tight shirt and pants that hugged her voluptuous body, and a matching apron tied around her waist.

"Oh, um, I'm actually waiting for someone," I stammered, feeling my cheeks heat up. My social awkwardness reared its head, as it often did when I was caught off guard.

"A date, huh?" she said, raising an eyebrow. "Well, I hope she's worth the wait. Or at least has the decency to text you if she's running late." Her words were playful, and her accent, a delightful mix of Spanish and American, made my heart flutter.

"Yeah, we confirmed the time and place," I mumbled, showing her our text conversation. Her fingers danced across my phone, scrolling through the messages. A frown crossed her face as she read, and then she looked up at me with a sympathetic smile.

"I hate to break it to you, but I think you've been ghosted, my friend. These replies are as cold as a margarita left out in the snow." Her humor, even in this awkward situation, was refreshing. I felt my shoulders relax as I realized she was right. I had been stood up.

"That's what I was afraid of," I sighed, feeling a mix of disappointment and relief. At least now I knew, and I didn't have to sit here wondering.

"Some people just don't have the guts to be honest," she said, her voice turning serious. "If it were me, I'd rather get it over with than leave someone hanging. You know, ghosting is for cowards."

I nodded, appreciating her honesty. "Well, at least I have these chips," I joked, trying to lighten the mood.

"Hey, if you want, I can get you a free drink to make up for the wasted time. On the house, of course," she offered, her brown eyes twinkling with kindness.

"No, that's okay. I should probably just head out," I said, feeling a bit dejected. I wasn't one to wallow in self-pity, but this stung a little more than I cared to admit.

"Suit yourself. But if you ever need a friendly face or some dating advice, you know where to find me," she said, giving me a warm smile. "I'm Emily, by the way."

"Cameron," I replied, mustering a smile. "Thanks, Emily. I might just take you up on that offer."

A week passed, and the memory of that failed date still lingered in my mind. I found myself back at Los Amigos, drawn to the familiar surroundings and the hope of seeing Emily again. As I entered, I scanned the bustling restaurant, and my heart skipped a beat when I spotted her. She was taking orders at a nearby table, her infectious laughter filling the room.

"Emily, over here!" I waved, feeling a bit nervous. I wasn't sure if she'd remember me, but I had to try.

Her eyes lit up when she saw me, and she made her way over, her hips swaying gracefully. "Cameron, fancy seeing you here again. Another date, or are you just a big fan of our chips and salsa?" Her playful banter made me smile.

"Well, I am a fan of the food, but I actually came back to see you," I blurted out, surprising myself with my boldness.

Emily's face softened, and she leaned in, lowering her voice. "Oh, really? And here I thought you were just another customer. What can I do for you, Cameron?"

I took a deep breath, gathering my courage. "I'm talking to another woman online, and I'm not sure if it's going anywhere. I was wondering if you could help me figure out if she's interested or not. You know, give me some dating advice."

Emily's eyes widened, and she bit her lip, considering my request. "I'm not sure I should get involved in your personal life, but I do love a good challenge. And I could use the extra cash. I get off in an hour. Meet me at the bar, and we can chat."

An hour later, I sat at the bar, nursing a margarita, when Emily appeared, looking stunning in a vibrant sundress that hugged her curves. Her dark hair cascaded over her shoulders, and her smile lit up the room.

"Wow, Emily, you look..." I trailed off, feeling my cheeks heat up again.

"I know, right? I can clean up pretty well when I'm not in this uniform," she said, twirling to show off her dress. "So, tell me about this online girl. What's the story?"

I took a sip of my drink, grateful for her help. "Well, we've been talking for a while, but I'm not sure if she's into me. I thought maybe you could help me figure out what I'm doing wrong."

Emily's eyes sparkled with determination. "Consider me your dating coach for the night. Let's see these messages."

As we scrolled through the conversation, Emily shook her head. "This girl is a dud, Cameron. She's not giving you much to work with here. You deserve someone who is more engaged and enthusiastic."

I sighed, feeling a mix of relief and disappointment. "I thought so, but I just wanted to be sure. I don't want to mess this up like the last time."

"Don't worry, my friend. There are plenty of fish in the sea, and we'll find you the right one. Maybe we should focus on personality more than looks. You know, go on a mock date, and I can help you work on your conversation skills."

I raised an eyebrow, intrigued by her suggestion. "A mock date? With you?"

Emily grinned, her eyes sparkling with mischief. "Why not? It'll be fun, and I can get to know you better. Who knows, maybe I'll even give you my number at the end of the night."

And so, our mock date began. We moved to a cozy booth, and over margaritas and delicious Mexican food, we swapped stories about our lives. I told her about my love for comic books and my dream of becoming a billionaire. She shared stories of her large, close-knit family and her passion for traveling, a dream often hindered by her financial situation.

As the night wore on, I found myself opening up to Emily in a way I never had with anyone else. She listened intently, her warm smile encouraging me to continue. I learned about her love for romantic movies and her talent for dancing, a skill she had honed since childhood. We laughed, we joked, and we connected on a level I had never experienced before.

When the restaurant began to empty out, I realized how late it had become. I didn't want the night to end, but I also didn't want to overstay my welcome.

"Well, Emily, this has been incredible," I said, feeling a mix of emotions. "I can't thank you enough for your help and for just being here."

Emily's eyes softened, and she reached across the table, taking my hand in hers. "Cameron, I had a wonderful time, too. You're sweet, and any girl would be lucky to have you."

My heart skipped a beat, and I leaned in, hoping for a kiss. But Emily pulled away, a playful smile on her lips. "But, I'm sorry, you're just not my type."

My heart sank, and I felt the familiar sting of rejection. "Oh, I see," I managed to say, my voice cracking.

Emily placed her hand on mine, her touch comforting. "Don't be sad, Cameron. I meant what I said. You're a great guy, and I'd love to help you find the right person. How about I be your official dating coach?"

I considered her offer, my mind racing with possibilities. "I'd like that, Emily. I really would. But I don't want to take advantage of your kindness."

"Nonsense," she said, waving away my concerns. "I enjoy spending time with you, and I get to help someone in the process. It's a win-win."

And just like that, a new chapter in my life began. Emily and I embarked on a journey of self-discovery, laughter, and the pursuit of love. Little did I know, the twists and turns our path would take, and the unexpected ways our relationship would grow.

Chapter 2

I stood at the entrance of my beach house, mesmerized by Emily's visit. The sun shone behind her, creating a radiant halo around her curvy figure, accentuated by the vibrant white sundress she wore. Her smile, warm and inviting, made my heart skip a beat. I couldn't help but notice the way the dress hugged her body, showcasing her ample bosom and generous hips. It was a stark contrast to my usual encounters with women, and I found myself captivated by her presence.

"Wow, Cameron, this place is incredible!" Emily exclaimed as she stepped inside, her eyes widening at the sight of the spacious living area. The oceanfront manor, my sanctuary, suddenly felt more vibrant with her lively spirit filling the air.

"Thanks, it's not much, just a place I call home," I replied, feeling a bit self-conscious about my wealth. I wasn't used to showing off my possessions, but Emily's reaction made me want to share more.

"Not much? This is huge!" She laughed, her voice echoing through the open-plan space. "You could fit my entire family in here and still have room for a dance party!"

I chuckled at her remark, feeling a warmth in my chest. "Well, I guess I like my space. And the view of the ocean is pretty amazing."

As Emily explored the house, her eyes darted around, taking in the modern furnishings and the floor-to-ceiling windows that offered breathtaking views of the beach. "This is like something out of a magazine! How did you afford all of this?"

Leaning against the kitchen counter, I explained, "I developed an algorithm for an AI app a few years back. It took off, and I made a decent amount of money from it. Enough to buy this place and invest in a few other ventures."

Emily's eyes widened further, and I could see the wheels turning in her head. "A millionaire, huh? And here I thought I was helping out a regular guy. You could've charged me for my own services!" She joked, playfully punching my arm.

I winced slightly at her touch, not because it hurt, but because it sent a tingling sensation through my body. "I'd never charge a friend, Emily. Besides, I need your help. You're the expert in this department."

She raised an eyebrow, her gaze intense. "Expert, huh? So, why does a millionaire need help getting a date? Shouldn't women be lining up for a chance to be with you?"

Sighing, I ran my hand through my afro, a nervous habit I had yet to break. "It's not about the money, Emily. Most of my life has been spent in front of a computer screen, coding and creating. I didn't have much time for socializing or dating. And after losing my parents last year..." My voice trailed off, the memory of their tragic accident still fresh in my mind.

Emily's playful demeanor softened, and she placed her hand on my arm, this time gently. "I'm so sorry about your parents, Cameron. I can't imagine what you've been through. Family is everything to me, and I don't know what I'd do if I lost one of them."

"I know," I said, feeling a connection with her that went beyond our initial encounter. "If I had a family like yours, I'd never let them out of my sight. It's just me, so I tend to keep to myself."

"Well, you're missing out on the good stuff," she teased, her smile returning. "My family can get a bit rowdy, but they're the best. You should come over for dinner one night. Just be prepared for the chaos."

The thought of spending time with her family intrigued me, and I found myself nodding in agreement. "I'd like that. Maybe I can get some tips on socializing from them."

Emily laughed, her eyes sparkling with mischief. "Oh, they'll love you! But let's focus on your dating life for now. Women love confidence, Cameron. You've got to believe in yourself and what you have to offer."

I shifted uncomfortably, feeling a bit vulnerable under her gaze. "I know, but it's not easy. I've never been good with women. I mean, I don't even know how to start a conversation without sounding like a total nerd."

"Nerdiness can be charming, trust me," she assured me, stepping closer. "But you need to update your approach. Going to a restaurant for a date is so old school. You need to do something fun, something that shows off your personality and interests."

Intrigued by her suggestion, I asked, "Like what? I'm not exactly the adventurous type."

Emily's eyes lit up with an idea. "How about paintball? You can never not have fun playing paintball. Take a date there, take some risk, have some fun, and you'll have plenty to talk about."

I couldn't help but smile at her suggestion. "That's actually brilliant! I've never thought of using my interests to my advantage. I know of a paintball area nearby."

"Perfect!" Emily clapped her hands excitedly. "Now, let's work on your profile picture. No more selfies in front of the computer, okay? We need something that showcases your best features."

She began to guide me through the house, suggesting different locations for photos. We ended up in the theater room, surrounded by my collection of comic books and movie memorabilia. "This is perfect! It shows your personality, and you can lean against that superhero statue like a cool, casual guy."

Posing for photos was not my forte, but with Emily's encouragement, I began to relax. She clicked away on her phone, capturing me in various poses. "You're a natural, Cameron! Just imagine you're the superhero in one of your favorite comics."

As the photo session progressed, I found myself enjoying Emily's company even more. Her laughter filled the room, and her playful banter made me feel at ease. I couldn't help but notice the way her sundress clung to her curves as she moved, and I felt a rush of desire, something I had never experienced before.

"Alright, Mr. Briggs, I think we've got enough material to work with," she said, reviewing the photos on her phone. "Now, let's talk about how to ask a woman out. It's all about confidence and making her feel special."

I listened intently as Emily shared her wisdom, her words resonating with me. "You need to make eye contact, Cameron. Look into her eyes and let her know you're interested. And don't be afraid to compliment her, but make it sincere."

Practicing the art of eye contact, I stared into Emily's deep brown eyes, getting lost in their warmth. "You have the most beautiful eyes, Emily. I could get lost in them."

She blushed, a charming pink hue spreading across her cheeks. "Oh, stop it. Remember what we said Cameron, just friends, remember?"

My heart raced, and I realized I was leaning closer to her, drawn to her like a moth to a flame. "Sorry, I'm just being honest. You're beautiful, and I..."

My words trailed off as I became aware of the distance between us shrinking. Emily's scent, a mix of flowers and something uniquely her, filled my senses. Before I knew it, our lips were inches apart, and I could feel her breath on my skin.

"Cameron," she whispered, her voice soft and inviting. "Friends?"

In that moment, I wanted nothing more than to kiss her. It was as if an electric current was flowing between us, urging me to take that leap. But something held me back, a voice in my head reminding me of my initial intentions.

"Sorry. I... I should probably get these photos sent to you," I stammered, breaking the spell. I stepped away, feeling a mix of emotions swirling within me.

Emily's expression softened, and she nodded, understanding my sudden change of heart. She fidgeted with her hair as if she too felt something. "It's okay. I'll text them to you right away. And we can work on your dating profile together."

As I retrieved my phone and texted with her, I couldn't shake the feeling that something significant had just happened. The connection between us was undeniable, but it was complicated by the fact that she was my dating coach and just a friend.

"I'll see you soon, Cameron," she said, her voice lingering in the air as she walked towards the door. "We'll get you ready for that paintball and find you the perfect date."

I watched as she left, her sundress swaying with each step. My mind raced with thoughts of what could have been and what might still be. Emily Lopez had become more than just a dating coach; she had become an integral part of my journey, and I was eager to see where this path would lead.

As the sun began its descent, casting a golden glow over the ocean, I sat on the plush outdoor sofa, reflecting on the day's events. My life had taken an unexpected turn, and I couldn't wait to see what the next chapter would bring. Perhaps, just perhaps, love and adventure were closer than I had ever imagined.

Chapter 3

After my transformative night with Emily, I was eager to apply her teachings and navigate this new dating terrain. Little did I know that this date would be a turning point in my journey, a step towards self-discovery and unexpected emotions.

I had met Abby a few days prior through a video chat arranged by a mutual friend. Her nerdy charm and bright personality had instantly captivated me. With her blonde hair, freckles, and a love for graphic tank tops, she was the epitome of a geek goddess. Our virtual conversation flowed effortlessly as we bonded over our shared interests in visual effects, video games, and Mexican food. It was as if I had found a kindred spirit in this vibrant woman.

As I got ready, I felt a sense of calm confidence, a feeling I rarely experienced when it came to social interactions. I dressed casually in my favorite jeans and a graphic t-shirt featuring a superhero I adored. I wanted to make a good impression, but Emily's advice echoed in my mind—be myself, and the right person will appreciate it. I took a deep breath, adjusted my glasses, and headed out, excited for the adventure that awaited me.

I arrived at the paintball arena, a bustling place filled with energetic players. My heart raced as I scanned the crowd, searching for Abby. And then, there she was, standing near the entrance, looking even more captivating in person. Her skinny frame was accentuated by a pair of ripped jean shorts and a colorful tank top, showcasing her unique style. Her glasses glinted in the sunlight, and her hair shimmered like golden rays. My nervousness dissipated as I approached her, feeling a connection that went beyond our shared love for all things nerdy.

"Abby, it's great to finally meet you in person!" I exclaimed, a wide smile spreading across my face.

"You too, Cameron!" she replied, her voice filled with enthusiasm. "I'm so glad we connected the other day. I had a feeling this would be fun."

Her warm greeting instantly put me at ease. We exchanged pleasantries, and I felt a spark of electricity as our eyes met. There was an unspoken understanding between us, a mutual appreciation for each other's company.

We spent the next few hours immersed in the exhilarating world of paintball. Abby's competitive spirit and quick reflexes impressed me. She moved with agility, dodging paintballs and strategizing like a pro. We formed an unbeatable team, capturing flags and outmaneuvering our opponents. The adrenaline rush of the game brought us closer, and I found myself laughing and enjoying the moment like never before.

As the day progressed, our conversation flowed effortlessly. We discovered even more common ground, from our favorite sci-fi franchises to our shared love for Mexican cuisine. Abby's passion for her work as a visual effects artist shone through, and I found myself hanging on her every word. She spoke about her dreams of creating groundbreaking special effects, and I couldn't help but admire her determination and talent.

After an intense final game, we decided to take a break and refuel. We headed to a nearby fast-food joint, a casual place known for its delicious chili hot dogs and milkshakes. We sat across from each other, our eyes sparkling with the excitement of the day.

"This has been the best date I've been on in ages, Cameron," Abby said, taking a bite of her chili dog. "Most guys would take me to fancy restaurants, but I love that you chose something fun and different."

Her words warmed my heart. I felt a sense of validation, knowing that my choice of activity had resonated with her. I smiled, recalling Emily's advice about finding unique ways to connect with someone.

"I'm glad you enjoyed it, Abby. I wanted to do something memorable, and I think paintball was a perfect choice," I replied, taking a sip of my milkshake.

"It was more than perfect," she said, her eyes twinkling. "I love that we can just be ourselves and have a great time. No pretenses, no expectations. It's refreshing."

I nodded in agreement, feeling a deep connection with her. We talked about our past relationships, our aspirations, and our love for adventure. Abby's openness and honesty were captivating, and I found myself sharing parts of my life I rarely spoke about. I told her about my parents' tragic accident and how it had shaped me. She listened intently, her eyes filled with empathy.

"I'm so sorry for your loss, Cameron," she said, reaching across the table and taking my hand. "It's incredible how you've managed to build such a successful career despite the hardships. You're an inspiration."

Her words touched me deeply. I felt a surge of emotions, a mix of sadness and gratitude. I realized that Abby saw beyond my awkwardness and appreciated the person I was.

"Thank you, Abby. It hasn't been easy, but I'm trying to make the most of life. And meeting someone like you makes it all worthwhile," I said, my voice cracking slightly.

Abby smiled, her eyes glistening with a hint of tears. "I feel the same way, Cameron. You're an amazing person, and I'm grateful to have met you."

The moment hung between us, heavy with unspoken emotions. I wanted to reach out and hold her, to feel the warmth of her touch. But I reminded myself of Emily's advice about taking things slow and not rushing into physical intimacy.

"Hey, I know we just met, but I was wondering if you'd like to go dancing this Saturday?" Abby asked, breaking the momentary silence. "There's this cool club in town that plays great music. I think you'd enjoy it."

I hesitated, recalling my aversion to dancing. It was one of my social fears, and I wasn't sure I was ready to face it just yet. But I didn't want to disappoint Abby, and I knew she loved dancing.

"I'm not much of a dancer, Abby. But if you really want to go, I'd be happy to join you," I said, mustering up my courage.

"Oh, that's amazing! I know you'll love it. It's a great way to let loose and have fun. And who knows, maybe you'll discover a hidden talent," she said, her eyes sparkling with excitement.

I smiled, feeling a mix of nervousness and anticipation. I had never considered myself a dancer, but the thought of sharing this experience with Abby made it seem less daunting.

As the evening drew to a close, we said our goodbyes, promising to meet again soon. I watched her walk away, her confident stride and playful demeanor leaving a lasting impression. I felt a sense of warmth and connection, something I hadn't experienced in a long time.

I walked home, my mind buzzing with thoughts of Abby. I couldn't believe how much I had enjoyed our date and how comfortable I felt with her. It was as if I had known her for years, yet there was still so much to discover. I was eager for our next encounter, to explore this newfound connection and see where it would lead.

As I lay in bed that night, I thought about Emily and her role in this unexpected turn of events. I was grateful for her guidance and the confidence she had instilled in me. But now, with Abby, I felt a different kind of excitement, a pull towards something more than just friendship. I wondered if this was the start of something special, a love story I had only read about in fantasy novels.

Chapter 4

I couldn't believe the turn of events as I stood there in my living room, gazing at Emily, the woman who had unexpectedly become a pivotal figure in my journey towards self-improvement and love. The revelation about my virginity seemed to have caught her off guard, but her reaction was far from what I'd anticipated.

"So, you're a virgin, huh?" Emily repeated, her dark eyes sparkling with a mixture of amusement and curiosity. Her thick, brunette hair bounced gently as she shook her head, a playful smile playing on her lips. "I guess that explains a lot."

I shifted uncomfortably, my skinny frame feeling gangly and awkward as I tucked my hands into the pockets of my jeans. "Yeah, I guess I never really got around to it. I mean, I had my priorities set on building my tech empire, and women... well, they weren't exactly lining up at my door." I offered a sheepish grin, my eyes fixating on the colorful superhero t-shirt I was wearing, the fabric stretching over my thin frame.

Emily let out a hearty laugh, her curvy figure shaking with mirth. "Oh, Cameron, you're something else! But I admire your dedication to waiting for the right person. It's rare these days." She took a step closer, her scent, a mixture of vanilla and cinnamon, enveloping me in its warmth. "So, what made you decide to take the plunge and start dating?"

I inhaled deeply, gathering my thoughts. "I realized that I was missing out on a big part of life. You know, I've achieved so much professionally, but my personal life has always been... lacking. I wanted to change that, and well, you were kind enough to offer your help." I gestured towards her, feeling a rush of gratitude for her presence in my life.

"And I'm glad I did!" She beamed, her eyes twinkling. "You know, Cameron, you're not like most guys. You're sweet, intelligent, and incredibly successful. Any woman would be lucky to have you." Her words sent a surge of warmth through my body, and I felt my cheeks flush under my dark skin.

"Really?" I asked, my voice cracking slightly. "I mean, I've never been great with women. I'm not exactly the smoothest talker, and my social skills..." I trailed off, my gaze drifting towards the floor.

"Hey, now," Emily interrupted, placing her hand gently on my arm. "You're doing great. I've seen how you've improved since we started this little journey. And trust me, with the right woman, your awkwardness can be endearing." She winked, her confidence in me boosting my spirits.

"So, you think Abby and I have a chance?" I asked, my heart skipping a beat at the mention of her name. Abby, the charming nerdy woman I'd met online, had captivated me from the moment we connected. Our date at the paintball arena had been exhilarating, and I couldn't deny the spark between us.

"Absolutely!" Emily exclaimed, her enthusiasm filling the room. "You two have so much in common, and from what you've told me, she seems to really like you. You should go for it, Cameron. Take a chance on love."

Her words resonated with me, and I felt a surge of determination. "I will," I declared, my voice steady and resolute. "I'm tired of playing it safe. It's time I stepped out of my comfort zone and took some risks."

Emily's face lit up with a radiant smile. "That's the spirit! And remember, dancing is a great way to loosen up and connect with your partner. It's all about feeling the music and letting go." She began swaying her hips to an imaginary beat, her curves moving in a mesmerizing rhythm.

I couldn't help but laugh, my nerves melting away under her infectious energy. "You make it sound so easy, but I'm telling you, my dancing skills are non-existent."

"Nonsense!" She laughed, taking my hands in hers. "Let me show you. Dancing is like a conversation between two bodies. You just need to find the right rhythm and go with the flow."

As she guided me through the spacious living room, I felt my anxiety dissipate. The music, a sultry Latin tune, filled the air, and Emily's body moved in perfect sync with the beat. I tried to mimic her movements, feeling awkward at first, but gradually, I began to relax and enjoy the rhythm.

Our bodies moved closer, and I felt the warmth of Emily's curves against mine. Her thick thighs brushed against my legs, and I could feel my heart racing. The sway of her hips and the gentle press of her breasts against my chest sent a rush of desire through me. I was acutely aware of her every movement, and my body responded instinctively.

Emily's eyes locked with mine, her gaze intense and filled with unspoken desires. I felt my breath quicken, and my hands instinctively found their way to her waist, pulling her closer. Her soft curves molded perfectly against my lean frame, and I could feel her breath on my neck, sending shivers down my spine.

As the song reached its climax, our bodies moved in perfect harmony, grinding against each other in a sensual dance. I felt my desires heighten, and I was acutely aware of my growing arousal. Emily's eyes glistened with a mixture of passion and hesitation, and I knew she felt the same electric connection.

Just as our lips were about to meet, Emily pulled away, breaking the spell. She coughed lightly, her cheeks flushed, and I realized we had crossed a line. The dance had become more than just a lesson; it was a moment of intense passion and desire.

"I... I should go," she stammered, taking a step back. "I... I have to get to work, and you have your date with Abby to prepare for." Her voice was shaky, and I could see the conflict in her eyes.

"Wait," I pleaded, reaching out to touch her arm. "Did I do something wrong? I thought we were..." I trailed off, not wanting to push her further.

Emily shook her head, a sad smile on her lips. "No, Cameron, you did nothing wrong. It's just... this is all happening so fast. I'm not sure I'm ready for this." She took a deep breath, her eyes filled with emotion. "I need to sort through my feelings. I'll see you later, okay?"

Before I could respond, she rushed out the door, leaving me alone in my living room, my heart pounding and my mind racing. I couldn't help but wonder what had just happened. The dance had been electric, and the connection between us was undeniable. But now, Emily was gone, leaving me with more questions than answers.

As I stood there, the silence of my oceanfront home enveloped me. I thought about Abby, the woman I was supposed to be focusing on. Our date was just days away, and I needed to ensure I was prepared. But my mind kept drifting back to Emily, her curves, and the unspoken desires that lingered between us.

I knew I had to get a hold of my emotions. The journey I had embarked on was not just about finding love; it was about self-discovery and growth. I had to learn to navigate these complex feelings and understand the dynamics of this unexpected love triangle.

With a determined mindset, I decided to focus on the present. I had a date to prepare for, and I was going to make it the best one yet. Abby deserved my full attention, and I was determined to show her the wonderful time she was hoping for.

As I sat down at my desk, my mind began to race with ideas for the perfect date. I wanted to create an experience that would showcase my creativity and thoughtfulness, something that would leave a lasting impression on Abby.

I thought back to our conversations, recalling her love for video games and her fascination with virtual reality. An idea began to form, and I smiled, feeling a surge of excitement. Perhaps, I could create a unique date experience that would combine her passions with mine, something that would truly showcase the potential of our connection.

I opened my laptop and began researching, my fingers flying across the keyboard as I delved into the world of virtual reality gaming. I wanted to create a customized adventure, a romantic quest tailored specifically for Abby. As I worked, my excitement grew, and I couldn't wait to see her reaction.

In the midst of my planning, my phone buzzed with a notification. It was a message from Emily.

"Hey, Cameron. I'm sorry about earlier. I just needed some time to process everything. I hope I didn't make you feel uncomfortable. I'll see you soon, okay? Take care."

I read the message twice, my heart aching at her words. Emily's presence in my life had become more significant than I'd anticipated, and now, I was left with the realization that my feelings for her were more complicated than I'd imagined.

With a heavy heart, I closed my laptop, knowing that my feelings for both women needed to be addressed. I was at a crossroads, and the path I chose would shape my future and the direction of this unexpected love triangle.

As the sun began to set, casting a golden glow over the ocean, I stood at the floor-to-ceiling windows, contemplating my next move. The journey of self-discovery had taken an unexpected turn, and I knew that the decisions I made from here on would not only affect my life but also the lives of two amazing women.

The story of my romantic quest was far from over, and the twists and turns that lay ahead promised to be both exhilarating and challenging. I took a deep breath, ready to embrace the unknown, for I knew that love, like life, was a daring adventure worth pursuing.

Chapter 5

I couldn't help but feel a surge of anticipation. Abby had agreed to come over to my place before our night out, and I was both nervous and excited to see her again. Our online connection had been electric, and our first date at the paintball arena had left me wanting more. I had no idea that someone like Abby, with her captivating personality and shared interests, could exist.

I smoothed down my shirt, feeling slightly self-conscious about my attire. Emily had insisted that I dress up for the occasion, hence the buttoned shirt, khakis and boat shoes, a departure from my usual graphic t-shirts, jeans, and sneaker's combo. I was still getting used to her dating advice, but so far, it had been a fascinating and helpful journey.

The sound of heels clicking on my driveway announced Abby's arrival. My breath caught in my throat as I walked off my porch to greet her. She looked stunning in a pink, low-cut mini dress that accentuated her slender figure. The dress hugged her in all the right places, and I couldn't help but notice how it enhanced her petite frame, making her look incredibly desirable. Her blonde hair framed her face, and the glasses she wore added a touch of intelligence to her overall look. Her hair blew from the ocean breeze and I could see the reflection of the bright moon on her glasses as she approached me.

"Wow, Abby, you look amazing," I blurted out, feeling my cheeks warm.

Abby grinned, her eyes sparkling with amusement. "Thanks, Cameron. You clean up pretty well yourself." She glanced at my outfit and gave me a playful wink.

I felt a rush of confidence, something I rarely experienced. I gestured towards my house, eager to show her around. "Welcome to my humble abode. I thought we could hang out here for a bit before heading out."

As we entered the house, I noticed Abby's eyes widening at the sight of the spacious interior. The floor-to-ceiling windows offered breathtaking views of the ocean, and the modern décor gave the place a sleek and sophisticated feel.

"This place is incredible," she exclaimed, her heels clicking on the wooden floor. "I love the open concept and the ocean views."

I smiled, feeling a sense of pride. "Thank you. I'm a bit of a tech geek, so I had fun incorporating some smart home features."

Abby's eyes lit up at the mention of tech. "Nerd." She mocked.

We both laughed at her quip as we both shared a love of technology.

I led her through the house, showing her the various rooms. We passed by the theater room, where she marveled at the candy bar and soda fountain, and the library, which housed my extensive collection of comic books and novels. But it was when we entered my home office that she let out a delighted squeal.

"Oh my, Cameron! Is this the video game you told me about?" She rushed over to the computer, her eyes glued to the screen.

I nodded, feeling a surge of satisfaction. "Yeah, I wanted to surprise you with it. It's not finished yet, but I thought you'd enjoy playing it. It's a fantasy RPG adventure. When I'm done you can customize your own character and go on different quests."

Abby's fingers flew across the keyboard, and soon she was immersed in the game. I stood behind her, watching as she effortlessly navigated through the virtual world I had created. Her enthusiasm was infectious, and I found myself grinning like a fool.

"This is amazing!" she exclaimed, her voice filled with excitement. "I love the graphics and the gameplay. You're really talented, Cameron."

Her words warmed my heart. I had spent countless hours working on the game, often forgetting to eat or sleep, driven by the desire to impress her. Hearing her praise meant the world to me.

"Thank you," I replied, my voice hoarse with emotion. "I wanted to make something special for you. I'm glad you like it."

Abby turned to face me, her expression softening. "I love it, Cameron. It's so thoughtful of you. But we should probably head out soon."

I nodded, feeling a twinge of disappointment that our gaming session had to end, but eager to spend more time with her. "Of course. We can always come back and play later."

As we made our way out of the house, I couldn't help but feel a sense of contentment. Seeing Abby enjoy my game and witnessing her genuine excitement had given me a boost of confidence. I was determined to make this date even more memorable.

We took a taxi from my private neighborhood to the bustling streets of the Virginia Beach oceanfront, stacked with various hotels and restaurants. We arrived at the nightclub, and the pulsating music and vibrant atmosphere instantly energized us. Abby's eyes lit up as she took in the surroundings, and I felt a rush of satisfaction, knowing I was about to dance with the most beautiful woman in the room.

"This is so much fun!" she shouted over the music, her eyes sparkling with excitement.

I grinned, feeling more at ease in this environment than I had expected. The dim lighting and crowded dance floor provided a sense of anonymity, allowing me to let loose and enjoy the moment.

After getting some drinks, Abby and I got on the dance floor and danced side by side. The entire time I thought of Emily and what she told me. I prayed I didn't look awkward doing the two step. However, after some time, I don't know if it was the alcohol or Abby's infectious behavior, I got into a groove and settled down.

We danced together for an hour, our bodies moving in sync to the beat. Abby's slender frame pressed against mine, and I could feel her warmth through the thin fabric of her dress. Her hair brushed against my face, and I inhaled her sweet scent, a mixture of cherry and something uniquely her.

As a song reached its climax, our bodies moved closer, and I felt a surge of desire. I leaned in, my lips inches from hers, ready to capture her mouth in a passionate kiss. But just as our lips were about to meet, Abby pulled away, her cheeks flushed.

"I need a break," she panted, fanning herself with her hand. "It's getting a little too hot in here."

I nodded, my heart pounding. "Yeah, sure. Let's get some air."

We made our way outside, and I could see that Abby was still flustered. Her cheeks were rosy, and she was breathing heavily. I wondered if it was the dancing or something more.

"Are you okay?" I asked, concerned. "Do you need some water?"

Abby shook her head, her glasses slightly askew. "I'm fine, just a bit lightheaded. Maybe it's the alcohol."

I wanted to believe her, but something in her eyes told me there was more to it. "Are you hungry? There's a great Mexican place nearby. We could grab a bite if you'd like."

At the mention of Mexican food, Abby's face lit up, and she grinned. "I love Mexican food! And I'm starving. Let's go."

I was thrilled that I could make her happy with such a simple suggestion. We headed to the restaurant, and as we walked in, I noticed a familiar face.

"Emily!" I called out.

Emily's eyes widened as she recognized me, and then her gaze shifted to Abby. She gave me a small smile, but it didn't reach her eyes. "Cameron, hi. I didn't know you were bringing a friend."

I introduced Abby to Emily, feeling a bit awkward about the situation. "Emily, this is Abby. Abby, Emily is a friend of mine. She works here."

Abby's eyes lit up with excitement. "It's so nice to meet you, Emily."

I could feel my cheeks burning, knowing I had never spoken about Emily to anyone. I had kept our unique relationship to myself, unsure of how to define it.

Emily's smile faltered for a moment, but she quickly recovered. "It's nice to meet you too, Abby. You two make a cute couple."

I could sense a hint of tension in her voice, but I wasn't sure why. I decided to ignore it, not wanting to ruin the evening.

We sat down in Emily's section, and she took our orders. As she walked away, I noticed Abby's curious gaze following her.

"She seems nice," Abby remarked. "You never told me you had a friend like her."

I shrugged, feeling a bit uncomfortable. "I guess I never really thought about it. Emily and I have a... unique relationship."

Abby's eyes sparkled with curiosity. "Unique? How so?"

I hesitated, unsure of how much to reveal. "Well, she's kind of my dating coach. She's been helping me navigate the dating world, giving me advice and tips."

Abby's eyes widened, and she let out a delighted laugh. "Oh my god, that's hilarious! I can't believe you have a dating coach. But it makes sense, considering your, um, social skills."

I felt a twinge of embarrassment, but I knew she was right. "Yeah, I'm not exactly a smooth talker when it comes to women. Emily's been a huge help."

As we enjoyed our meal, I couldn't shake the feeling that something was bothering Emily. I noticed her stealing glances at us, her expression unreadable. I decided to call her later to check in, hoping to understand her reaction.

After dinner, Abby and I headed back to the nightclub, determined to make the most of our night. We danced, laughed, and shared stories, creating memories that would stay with me for a long time.

As the night drew to a close, I walked Abby to her car, feeling a mix of emotions. I wanted to kiss her, to express my growing feelings, but I held back, not wanting to rush things.

"I had an amazing time tonight, Cameron," Abby said, her voice soft and dreamy. "Thank you for everything."

"The pleasure was all mine," I replied, meaning every word. "I can't wait to see you again."

We shared a lingering hug, and I watched as she drove away, feeling a sense of contentment and anticipation for what the future might hold.

Later that night, I found myself dialing Emily's number, unable to shake the feeling that something was amiss. She picked up on the third ring, her voice groggy.

"Cameron? What's wrong? It's late," she said, her tone guarded.

"I'm sorry to call so late, but I wanted to check on you. You seemed a bit off tonight at the restaurant," I explained.

There was a pause, and I could almost hear Emily's thoughts whirring. "I'm fine, Cameron. Just tired, I guess. It was a long shift."

I wasn't convinced, but I didn't want to push. "Well, I just wanted to make sure. I appreciate everything you've done for me, Emily. You've been a great friend."

Emily sighed, and I could sense her frustration. "We aren't friends, Cameron. Not really. We had a deal, remember? I was helping you get a date. And you got one. With Abby."

Her words hit me like a ton of bricks. I had never thought of our relationship in those terms. "But I thought..."

"You thought what, Cameron?" Emily's voice was sharp now. "That I'd be your friend forever? That I'd stick around even after you found someone?"

I was stunned by her reaction. "I... I don't know. I just thought we had a connection."

"We had a deal, Cameron," Emily said, her voice softening. "It always about you finding love. And you have. With Abby. Maybe it's time to let me go."

I felt a knot in my throat, not wanting to accept the reality of the situation. "But I..."

"It's okay, Cameron," Emily interrupted gently. "You don't owe me anything. I'm glad I could help. And I'm happy for you. Good night."

Before I could respond, the line went dead. I stood there, phone in hand, feeling a mix of emotions. Confusion, hurt, and a sense of loss washed over me. I had never expected our relationship to end like this.

As I lay in bed that night, my mind raced with thoughts of Emily and Abby. I couldn't help but question my feelings for both women. Was I falling for Abby, the charming nerd who shared my interests? Or was there something more to my connection with Emily, the vibrant, outgoing woman who had become my unexpected friend and dating coach?

The thought of losing Emily, even if it meant finding love with Abby, left me with a hollow feeling. I had never expected to form such a strong bond with her, and now I was faced with the realization that our relationship might be coming to an end.

Chapter 6

The anticipation had been building ever since our prior two dates, and I couldn't wait to see Abby again. I had to admit, I was nervous, but this time, it was different. I found myself looking forward to her arrival, eager to spend more time with her and continue the connection we had forged. As I stood in my spacious kitchen, preparing a special dinner for us, I felt a surge of excitement. I had opted for a classic steak dinner with all the trimmings, hoping to impress Abby with my culinary skills. The aroma of garlic and herbs filled the air as I sautéed green beans on the stove, while the mashed potatoes simmered in a pot, their steam fogging up my glasses.

Through the kitchen's open concept, I could see the vast ocean stretching to the horizon, the waves crashing against the sand in a soothing rhythm. My home, a modern beachfront sanctuary, provided the perfect backdrop for a romantic evening. The floor-to-ceiling windows in the living room showcased the breathtaking view, and the setting sun painted the sky with hues of orange and pink.

Just as I was about to check on the steaks, I heard the front door open, and my heart skipped a beat. Abby had arrived, and the sound of her voice as she called out my name sent a thrill through me. I wiped my hands on a kitchen towel and turned to greet her, a wide smile spreading across my face.

Abby stood in the entryway, looking adorable as always. She wore a tank top featuring a superhero I recognized from one of my favorite comic book series, paired with ripped jean shorts that accentuated her slender legs. Her blonde hair, tied back in a messy ponytail, framed her delicate features, and her glasses rested on the bridge of her nose. Her attire perfectly complemented the various superhero paintings adorning the walls of my home.

"You know I still can't get how incredible this place is. It's like a geek's wet dream!" she exclaimed, her eyes widening as she took in the spacious living area. "And the view... it's breathtaking!"

"Thanks," I replied, feeling a sense of pride in my home. "I'm glad you like it. Make yourself comfortable. Can I get you something to drink? Maybe some wine?"

"Wine sounds perfect," she said, walking towards the kitchen. "I have to say, I'm impressed with your taste in art. You know how jealous I am of your X-men statues. They're my favorite superheroes, too!"

I chuckled, moving to the wine fridge and pulling out a bottle of red. "Mine as well. I got that statues at a comic convention a few years back. It's one of my prized possessions."

As I poured the wine into two glasses, I felt a sense of ease in Abby's presence. It was as if we had known each other for years, and the awkwardness I usually experienced around women seemed to fade away. During dinner, we chatted about our shared love for superheroes. The conversation flowed so easily with her. It didn't feel like I was talking to a date. Instead, it felt like I was talking to a friend.

After dinner, I showed her the rest of my collection, in my library, which included rare comic books and limited-edition figurines. She followed me around the vast space with multiple books, reading the titles of some of my favorite artists. I smiled watching her, as she sipped her wine and flipped through a few pages of a comic book she found.

"Your collection is amazing, Cameron," she said, her eyes sparkling with excitement. "It's like a mini-museum! I can't believe you have the first edition of this X-Men comic too. I've been searching for it forever!"

I smiled, feeling a rush of pleasure at her enthusiasm. "I'm happy to share my passion with someone who appreciates it. Not many people understand the significance of these collectibles."

Abby took a sip of her wine, her eyes glancing around the library. "It's incredible, and I love how you've incorporated your interests into your home. It's so... you."

Her words warmed my heart. I had always felt like an outsider, but with Abby, I felt understood and accepted. As we finished our walk around the house, we ended up in the theater room, where I had set up a cozy movie night. The original X-Men movie, one of our mutual favorites, was cued up, and a bowl of freshly popped popcorn sat on the table, along with various candies and snacks.

"This is amazing!" Abby exclaimed, taking in the theater's amenities. "A popcorn maker, a candy bar, and a soda fountain? You've thought of everything!"

I shrugged, feeling a bit embarrassed by my indulgence. "I love movies, and I wanted to create the ultimate viewing experience. I'm glad you like it."

As the movie started, we settled into the plush recliners, our feet propped up on the extended footrests. The room darkened, and the only light came from the screen, casting a warm glow on Abby's face. I couldn't help but admire her, the way her eyes lit up with excitement during the action scenes, and how she mouthed the words to the characters' dialogue.

Midway through the movie, Abby scooted closer to me, her shoulder brushing against mine. I held my breath, my heart pounding in my chest. This was the moment I had been both dreading and anticipating. I knew I had to tell her the truth, but I was afraid of how she would react.

Abby leaned her head on my shoulder, her blonde hair tickling my cheek. I stiffened, unsure of how to respond. She must have sensed my hesitation because she lifted her head and looked at me with concern.

"Did I do something wrong?" she asked, her voice soft and gentle. "I'm sorry if I made you uncomfortable."

I shook my head, forcing a smile. "No, it's not that. It's just... I'm not used to this, that's all."

"Not used to what?" she probed, her eyes searching mine.

I took a deep breath, steeling myself for her reaction. "I'm... I'm a virgin, Abby. I've never been in a relationship before, and I've never..." I trailed off, feeling my face heat up.

Abby's eyes widened, and for a moment, I thought I saw disappointment flash across her face. But then, she reached out and placed her hand on mine, giving it a gentle squeeze.

"It's okay, Cameron," she said, her voice filled with kindness. "I respect your decision to wait. You're a good guy, and guys like you are hard to come by these days."

Relief washed over me, and I felt a weight lift from my shoulders. I hadn't expected her to react so positively, and I was grateful for her understanding.

"I really like you, Cameron," she continued, her voice softening. "Your kind, and you've shown me a wonderful time. I hope you know that I..." She trailed off, biting her lip, as if debating whether to say more.

I felt my heart flutter in my chest. I wanted to hear what she had to say, but at the same time, I was afraid. Afraid of getting hurt, of opening up and exposing my vulnerable self. But Abby's gaze, filled with warmth and sincerity, urged me to take a chance.

"I like you, too, Abby," I confessed, my voice barely above a whisper. "I've enjoyed our time together, and I..." I paused, searching for the right words. "I want to kiss you, but I don't know if it's the right time."

Abby's eyes widened, and a soft smile played on her lips. "It's always the right time if it feels right," she said, her voice barely audible over the movie's soundtrack.

Without another word, I leaned in, closing the distance between us. Our lips met in a gentle kiss, soft and tentative at first, but soon deepening as we surrendered to the moment. Her lips were warm and sweet, and I felt a rush of desire coursing through my veins.

As we pulled apart, breathless, Abby rested her forehead against mine, her eyes sparkling with amusement. "Well, that was a nice surprise," she said, her voice laced with a hint of mischief.

I felt a surge of confidence, a feeling I had never experienced before. "I'm glad you think so," I replied, my voice hoarse with emotion. "I've been wanting to do that since our first date."

Abby giggled, her eyes twinkling with happiness. "I'm glad you finally did. I've been hoping for this, too."

The rest of the movie passed in a blur, and before I knew it, the credits were rolling. We had spent the remainder of the evening cuddled up on the recliners, sharing stories and getting to know each other on a deeper level. It was as if we had known each other for years, and yet, there was still so much to discover.

As the night drew to a close, Abby stood up, stretching her arms above her head. "I should probably head home," she said, a hint of reluctance in her voice. "But I had a wonderful time, Cameron. Thank you for a perfect evening."

I walked her to the front door, my heart heavy at the thought of her leaving. I wanted to ask her to stay, to spend the night and wake up beside her, but I didn't want to come on too strong.

"I'll walk you out," I said, opening the door and stepping onto the porch. The night air was cool, and the moon cast a silvery glow on the ocean waves.

Abby turned to face me, her eyes shining in the moonlight. "I had a great time, too. I can't wait to see you again."

I smiled, feeling a surge of happiness. "Me too. How about we go out again soon? Maybe to the renaissance festival in town."

"I'd like that," she said, her voice filled with anticipation. "I'll see you soon, Cameron."

I watched as she walked to her car, her slender figure illuminated by the porch light. As she drove away, I felt a mixture of emotions. I was excited about the prospect of our next date, but I couldn't shake the feeling that I had missed an opportunity to take our relationship to the next level.

I made a promise to myself then and there, that the next time we were together, I would seize the moment and let my feelings guide me. I wanted to explore this connection with Abby, to see where it would lead, and I was determined to make it work, no matter what challenges lay ahead.

Little did I know, our journey was about to take an unexpected turn, one that would test my resolve and change the course of my life in ways I could never have imagined.

Chapter 7

As the morning sun shone brightly, I eagerly awaited Abby's arrival for our adventure to the Renaissance Festival. I had never been to one before, but Abby's enthusiasm for all things medieval was infectious, and I found myself getting caught up in her excitement. I wanted to impress her, so I suggested we attend the festival together, a perfect blend of her love for history and my desire to create memorable experiences.

I watched out the window, my heart fluttering with anticipation as her car pulled into the driveway. She stepped out, and my breath caught in my throat. Abby looked stunning in a medieval-inspired outfit—a tight corset accentuating her slender waist, a short skirt revealing her long, pale thighs, and a pair of leather boots that reached her knees. Her blonde hair, loose and flowing, framed her face, and her glasses added a touch of intelligence to her playful ensemble.

"Wow, Cameron, you look..." Abby's voice trailed off as she took in my appearance. I had tried my best to dress the part, donning a pair of tights and a loose-fitting blouse, feeling a bit foolish but willing to embrace the experience. "You look... dashing," she finally said, a playful smile on her lips.

I felt my cheeks warm under her gaze. "You think so? I feel a bit ridiculous, to be honest." I adjusted my clothing, feeling self-conscious, but Abby's laughter eased my nerves.

"No, you look great! I love the effort you put into this. It's like you stepped right out of a history book." She stepped closer, her eyes sparkling with mischief. "And I must say, those tights do wonderful things for your legs."

I felt a rush of heat between my thighs at her words. "Oh, well, I can't take all the credit. They're a bit tight, to be honest." I laughed, trying to hide my sudden arousal. I wasn't used to someone like Abby, who made me feel both nervous and desired.

Abby's fingers lightly traced the fabric of my blouse, her touch sending shivers down my spine. "I like it. It shows off your muscles." She gently squeezed my bicep, and I could swear my knees weakened. "You're a sexy nerd, Cameron. Own it."

Her words surprised me, and I felt a surge of confidence. "Well, if you insist," I replied, trying to sound nonchalant. "I'm glad you approve of my... fashion choices."

"Oh, I do. And I can't wait to show you off at the festival," she said, her eyes twinkling. "Let's go, my knight in not-so-shining armor."

We drove to the festival grounds, chatting excitedly about the day ahead. The festival was bustling with activity, filled with colorful tents, lively music, and people dressed in all manner of medieval attire. We wandered through the marketplace, sampling exotic foods, watching street performers, and admiring the intricate crafts on display.

Abby's eyes lit up as we approached a jousting arena. "Oh, I love this! We have to watch a match. It's so exciting!" She dragged me through the crowd, her enthusiasm contagious. We found a spot near the front, and I couldn't help but stare at her, her eyes gleaming with childlike wonder.

The joust began, and the crowd roared with each clash of lances. Abby cheered wildly, her pale skin flushed with excitement. I found myself getting caught up in the action, feeling my heart race as the knights battled. When the victor was declared, Abby turned to me, her eyes sparkling.

"That was amazing! I love the thrill of it all. I feel like I've been transported back in time." She leaned closer, her breath warm on my neck. "I'm so glad we came here, Cameron. This is the best date ever."

I felt my cheeks flush at her words. "It is pretty incredible. I'm glad I could share this with you." I paused, taking in her beauty. "You look amazing, by the way. I love this outfit on you."

Abby's cheeks pinked, and she played with the lace of her corset. "Thanks. I wanted to look good for you. I mean, I know it's a bit over the top, but I thought, why not embrace the theme?"

"It's perfect," I assured her, reaching out to touch her hand. "And I'm glad you did. You look beautiful, and I feel like the luckiest guy here."

As the day progressed, we tried our hand at various activities. We cheered on sword fighters, laughed as we attempted to throw axes (with little success), and devoured juicy turkey legs, juices dripping down our chins. The festival was a sensory overload, filled with sights, sounds, and smells that transported us to another era.

Dark storm clouds began to gather, casting a shadow over the festival. Abby and I looked at each other, surprised, as we hadn't checked the weather forecast. "I didn't think it was supposed to rain," she said, her voice laced with concern.

Before we could seek shelter, the sky opened up, and a torrential downpour drenched us. We ran for cover, laughing at our misfortune, our clothes clinging to our bodies. The rain showed no signs of letting up, so we decided to head back to my place, both of us shivering from the cold.

Once we arrived, I quickly lit a fire in the fireplace to warm up the room. Abby and I stripped off our wet clothes, leaving them in a pile by the hearth. It was hard not to ogle her in her matching black bra and panties, but I managed to control my and go to my room for fresh clothes. Returning back to the living room, I handed her a pair of my sweatpants and an oversized t-shirt, feeling a bit awkward but wanting to make her comfortable.

"Here, these should fit you," I said, my voice cracking slightly. "I'll just throw these in the dryer to get them warm and dry."

Abby took the clothes, her slender fingers brushing against mine, sending a jolt of electricity through my body. "Thanks, Cameron. I really appreciate this." She disappeared into the bathroom, and I tried to focus on the task at hand, my mind racing with thoughts of her in my clothes.

I returned with the warm clothes, finding Abby curled up on the couch, the fire crackling nearby. She looked cozy and adorable, her blonde hair spilling over the soft fabric of my shirt.

"I had so much fun today," she said, a smile playing on her lips. "It was one of the best dates I've been on. Thank you for suggesting it."

"I'm glad you enjoyed it," I replied, sitting next to her. "I did too. It was... different, but in a good way. And I love seeing you in my clothes." I blushed, realizing how that might have sounded.

Abby giggled, her eyes sparkling with mischief. "Yeah, I bet you do. They're pretty big on me, but they're comfy." She snuggled closer, her body warm against mine. "I like being here with you, Cameron. It feels... right."

I turned to face her, our eyes locking. "It does, doesn't it? I mean, I've enjoyed our time together, and I..." I paused, my heart pounding in my chest. "I think I'm falling for you, Abby."

Her eyes widened, and she placed a gentle hand on my cheek. "Cameron, I... I feel the same. I didn't expect this, but I think I'm falling for you too."

Without another word, I leaned in, capturing her lips with mine. The kiss was soft and tender at first, our mouths moving in sync, exploring each other gently. I tasted the sweetness of her lips, and my hands found their way to her waist, pulling her closer.

Abby responded with passion, her tongue meeting mine in a dance of desire. Her hands roamed over my body, exploring the muscles beneath the thin fabric of my t-shirt. I could feel her hardening nipples pressing against my chest, and my cock twitched in response.

I wanted to touch her, to feel her soft skin under my fingers. I slid my hands under the baggy shirt, my palms gliding over her flat stomach, enjoying the feel of her warm flesh. Abby moaned into my mouth, her hands tugging at my shirt, urging me to take it off.

Eager to please her, I lifted my arms, allowing her to pull the shirt over my head. Her eyes widened as she took in my bare chest, her fingers tracing the contours of my muscles. "You're so sexy, Cameron," she whispered, her breath hot on my skin.

I shivered at her touch, my cock straining against the sweatpants. I wanted to feel her body against mine, to be as close as possible. I kissed her deeply, my hands moving to the hem of her borrowed shirt, slowly lifting it up. Abby raised her arms, letting me pull it off, revealing her delicate lace bra and her small, firm breasts.

"You're so beautiful," I breathed, my voice hoarse with desire. I cupped her breasts, my thumbs brushing over her erect nipples, eliciting a soft moan from her. "I want to touch you everywhere."

Abby's hands found the drawstring of my pants, her fingers fumbling as she tried to undo it. My cock twitched as her fingers were a mere inch away. I didn't know if we were going to have sex, but I wanted to.

As we kissed, content in each other's arms, the sound of my phone ringing startled us.

"Shit," she growled. "I'm sorry I have to check my phone. Pause this moment?"

"Sure."

Abby smiled and kissed me once more before reaching for her phone. As soon as she saw the screen, her expression changed as she answered the call.

"Hello? Oh, it's you..." Her voice trailed off, and I could see the conflict in her eyes. "Yes, I understand. I'll be there as soon as I can." She ended the call, her face a mix of frustration and determination.

"What is it? Is everything okay?" I asked, concerned.

Abby took a deep breath, her eyes filled with regret. "That was my business partner. There's an emergency with a big project, and I need to go to Los Angeles immediately. I have to leave right now."

My heart sank at her words. "Oh, Abby, I'm so sorry."

She shook her head, her eyes glistening with unshed tears. "I just... I need to go, and I don't know when I'll be back."

I understood the importance of her work, but my heart ached at the thought of her leaving. "I get it. Work is important. But where does this leave us?"

Abby bit her lip, her eyes searching mine. "I don't know, Cameron. I hate long-distance relationships. They never work. But I can't just... I need to do this. For me. My career I've worked so hard to get where I am."

I nodded, my throat tight with emotion. "I understand. I don't want to hold you back. You should go and take care of your business. But know that I'll be here when you get back."

Abby leaned in, her lips brushing mine softly. "Thank you for understanding. I'm sorry to leave like this, but I promise, if I return and you're still single, we can pick up right where we left off. You're a great guy, Cameron. I feel like such an ass to leave now, especially after what we just experienced."

I pulled her into a tight embrace, my heart heavy. "It's okay. I'll be here. And I'll be waiting for you."

Abby kissed me once more, her lips lingering on mine. "I have to go. Can I keep the outfit? I'll mail it back when I can."

"Keep it," I said, my voice hoarse. "It looks better on you anyway."

She smiled sadly, her eyes glistening. "You're too good to me. I fucking hate my job right now."

I watched as she gathered her things, her wet clothes in a bag, and headed for the door. I stood there, feeling a sense of loss as she waved goodbye, the door closing behind her.

Slumping onto the couch, I stared into the dying embers of the fire, my mind reeling. Had I just lost the most amazing woman I'd ever met? Would she come back? And if she did, would I still be waiting for her? The uncertainty of our future hung heavy in the air, leaving me with more questions than answers.

Chapter 8

I couldn't help but feel a sense of loneliness as I walked into Los Amigos, the familiar scent of Mexican spices filling my nostrils. It had been a few weeks since my date with Abby, and our abrupt farewell still lingered in my mind. The Renaissance Festival had been magical, but the abrupt end to our night had left me with more questions than answers. I never imagined that our passionate evening would be cut short by a work emergency, sending Abby rushing off to Los Angeles. We had agreed to stay in touch, but the distance between us now felt like an insurmountable obstacle.

Seeking solace and perhaps some much-needed advice, I found myself at the same restaurant where I had first met Emily, my dating coach, and confidant. As I approached the bar, I spotted her through the crowd, her brunette hair cascading over her shoulders as she laughed with a group of colleagues. I hesitated, wondering if I should interrupt her work break, but my desire for guidance outweighed my reservations.

"Hey Emily," I called out. She turned, her dark eyes meeting mine, and a smile spread across her face.

"Cameron! What a surprise. I thought I told you not to come back here," she teased, her tone playful.

"I know, I know. But I need your help again," I pleaded, my voice laced with desperation. "I'm not sure what happened with Abby. We had this amazing date at the Renaissance Festival, but then she got a work call and had to leave for LA. Now, I don't know if we're even still together."

Emily's smile faded, replaced by a look of concern. "Oh, honey. That's rough. Are you broken up?"

I sighed, running my hand through my curly afro. "I don't know. She said we could still be friends, but I don't want to just be friends. We had something special, I think."

Emily placed her hand on my arm, her touch comforting. "I'm sorry, Cameron. From the sound of things it sounds like you're broken up."

"Fuck..." I snapped, placing my hands on my face. "How can I ever find love now?"

"You're a good guy, Cameron. There are plenty of fish in the sea. You'll find someone else."

Her words offered little solace, but I appreciated her attempt to cheer me up. "Thanks, but it's not that easy. I mean, I'm a virgin, and I thought Abby was the one. Now I'm back to square one."

A spark of determination ignited in Emily's eyes. "Well, if you're looking for a fresh start, I might know just the thing."

Intrigued, I leaned closer. "What do you have in mind?"

She bit her lip, a mischievous glint in her eye. "My family is having a house party tonight. It's a big get-together, lots of food, music, and dancing. You should come. It'll be fun, and who knows, maybe you'll meet someone new."

The thought of attending a party with Emily's family was both exciting and terrifying. I had always been socially awkward, and large gatherings made me nervous. But the prospect of moving on and potentially meeting someone new was enticing.

"Okay, I'll go," I agreed, surprising myself with my boldness. "But only if you promise to stick by my side. I'm not great with crowds."

Emily's eyes lit up, and she squeezed my arm playfully. "Deal! I'll be your wingwoman for the night. We'll have a blast."

As the sun began its descent, I found myself standing on the doorstep of Emily's family home, my heart pounding in my chest. The sound of laughter and music filled the air, and the delicious aroma of homemade Mexican food wafted through the open windows. Emily, had changed and was dressed in a vibrant floral dress that hugged her curves. She took my hand and led me inside.

"Everyone, this is my friend Cameron!" she announced, her voice ringing with pride.

The room fell silent for a brief moment as all eyes turned towards me. I felt my face heat up under their scrutiny, but Emily's reassuring smile kept me grounded.

"Is he your new boyfriend?" a playful voice called out from the crowd.

Emily's cheeks flushed, and she quickly shook her head. "No, no. We're just friends. Cameron, meet my family."

I was introduced to a sea of smiling faces, each one welcoming me with open arms. Emily's family was as vibrant and lively as she was, and they made me feel right at home. We mingled, ate, and laughed, and as the night progressed, I found myself relaxing and enjoying the festivities.

As the night progressed, Emily and I made our way to the dance floor. At first I didn't want to dance, but with curves like hers it was hard to say no.

Emily and I danced together, our bodies moving in sync to the upbeat Latin music. Her hips swayed gracefully, and I found myself drawn to her every move. Our eyes locked, and I felt a spark of electricity pass between us. The sexual tension was palpable, and as we danced closer, our lips nearly touching, I could feel my heart racing.

"It's hot in here," Emily breathed, fanning herself with her hand. "Let's get some air."

We stepped outside into the cool night air, our bodies still buzzing from the sensual dance. Emily leaned against the porch railing, her chest rising and falling with each breath. I stood beside her, my eyes tracing the curves of her body, illuminated by the soft glow of the moon.

"That was fun," I said, my voice hoarse with desire.

Emily's eyes met mine, and she took a step closer. "Yeah, it was."

Before I could process what was happening, her lips were on mine, soft and warm. I kissed her back, my hands finding their way to her waist, pulling her closer. It was a kiss fueled by passion and longing, and I couldn't get enough.

She pulled away, her breath ragged. "Shit, I didn't mean to do that. I'm sorry, Cameron."

Confused by her sudden retreat, I reached for her hand. "It's okay. I wanted to kiss you too."

Emily's eyes searched mine, a mix of emotions playing across her face. "I know this is complicated. I know you feelings with Abby are still raw, and I shouldn't cross that line."

"I don't care about that," I said, my voice low and steady. "I want this, Emily. I want you."

A silent battle waged within her, and then she nodded, her decision made. "Come on, let's get out of here."

We hurriedly said our goodbyes to her family, making our way to the waiting taxi. The ride back to her place was filled with anticipation and unspoken desires. As we entered her apartment, Emily grabbed a bottle of tequila from the kitchen, a mischievous smile on her face.

"Here's to breaking the rules," she said, pouring us each a shot.

We clinked glasses and downed the tequila, the fiery liquid burning its way down my throat. Emily kicked off her sandals and sat on the couch, and I sat down beside her.

"Come here..." she pulled me close, and we made out once more.

I grinned and kissed her again. I really liked kissing her. Her smooth soft lips felt like pillows as we deepened our desires for each other grew. Emily reached out and touched the outline of my hard cock in my jeans and i shivered.

"Are you okay?" She asked.

"I've never done this before," I admitted, my voice laced with nervousness.

Emily's eyes softened. "I know. But I'm here for you, Cameron. I want this to be special."

I took a deep breath, my heart pounding in my chest. "I want it to be special too."

Emily leaned in, her lips brushing against my ear, sending shivers down my spine. "Let's take it slow. I want to make sure you enjoy every moment."

Her hands found the hem of my shirt, and with gentle fingers, she began to lift it over my head. I raised my arms, my skin tingling with anticipation. Emily's eyes widened as she took in the sight of my bare chest, her fingers tracing the contours of my muscles.

"You're gorgeous," she whispered, her breath hot against my skin.

I reached for her, pulling her close, and our lips met in a hungry kiss. Our tongues danced, exploring each other with growing urgency. Emily's hands roamed my body, igniting a fire within me. She unbuttoned my jeans, her fingers brushing against my rock-hard cock through my boxers.

"Wait," she said, her voice breathless. "We need to use protection. I don't want any accidents."

I nodded, my mind clouded with desire. "Yeah, of course."

Emily left the living room, to go into her bedroom and when she returned, she was naked and had a condom in her hands. My cock twitched ogling her nude figure. I especially liked her big breasts, and smooth thick thighs. Emily sat next to me on the couch, her hands shaking slightly as she tore open the packet. She sheathed me, her touch sending sparks of pleasure through my body. I watched, mesmerized, as she straddled me, her curvy figure above me.

"Are you sure you're ready?" she asked, her eyes searching mine.

I nodded, my heart pounding. "I'm sure. I want you, Emily."

With a slow, deliberate motion, she lowered herself onto me, her warmth enveloping me. I groaned, the sensation overwhelming. Emily began to move, her hips undulating in a rhythmic dance, her large breasts swaying with each bounce. I ran my hands up her tan thick thighs, feeling the softness of her skin, my fingers dipping into the wetness between her legs.

"Oh, Cameron," she moaned, her head thrown back in pleasure. "You feel so good."

“Really?” I breathed.

She nodded and kissed me once more. As she rode me, she smiled, “guess what?”

“What?” I moaned enjoying the pleasures of her smooth pussy milking my cock.

“You're no longer a virgin.”

“Oh, yeah...”

“Yes, papi.”

“Does it feel good?”

“Yes, I love your cock. It feels good in me papi. Real good.” She sensually kissed me as we drifted in the moment of our sexual bliss.

I matched her rhythm, my body moving in sync with hers. The pleasure built, each thrust sending me closer to the edge. Emily's eyes fluttered shut, her mouth parted in a silent cry as she rode me. She muttered in words in Spanish as her pleasure grew. I smiled, thinking it was sexy. I reached up, cupping her full breasts, my thumbs brushing her nipples, eliciting a sharp gasp from her.

"I'm close," she whispered, her voice breathy. "I want you to come with me. Fuck me. Thrust your hips into me."

I felt my orgasm building, an intense pressure coiling in my groin. I thrust harder, my body on the brink of release. Emily's hands gripped my shoulders, her nails digging into my skin as she climaxed, her walls pulsing around me.

"Oh, fuck!" she cried out, her body trembling.

I couldn't hold back any longer. With a final, powerful thrust, I erupted inside her, filling the condom, my body shaking with the force of my release. Emily collapsed onto my chest, her breath coming in ragged gasps. We lay entwined, our hearts racing, our bodies slick with sweat.

"That was incredible," I whispered, my lips brushing her ear.

Emily lifted her head, her eyes sparkling with satisfaction. "It was. How was your first time?"

"Amazing." I grinned.

"And it's just the beginning, Cameron. I want to show you so much more."

A wave of contentment washed over me, and I knew in that moment that I had made the right choice. Emily was more than a dating coach; she was a woman who understood me, who wanted me, and who was willing to guide me through this new, exhilarating chapter of my life.

As we lay there, our bodies still intertwined, I couldn't help but wonder what the future held for us. I had finally taken a leap of faith, and now, with Emily by my side, I was ready to embrace the unknown, eager to explore the depths of desire and discover the possibilities that lay ahead.

Chapter 9

I woke up with a goofy grin on my face, my eyes adjusting to the morning sunlight streaming through the bedroom window. There she was, Emily, lying naked beside me, her tanned skin glowing in the warm light. Her dark hair fanned out on the pillow, contrasting beautifully with her fair complexion. I couldn't take my eyes off her plus sized curves, the gentle rise and fall of her large breasts with each breath, and the soft roundness of her thick hips. It was hard to believe that just a few hours ago, she had taken my virginity, and now here we were, tangled in the sheets, our bodies still buzzing with the afterglow of passion.

I felt a surge of satisfaction, mixed with a hint of regret. A part of me wished I had discovered this side of myself sooner, but the timing felt right with Emily. She had been patient and understanding, guiding me through my first sexual experience with care and passion. I reached out, tracing the line of her shoulder with my finger, enjoying the softness of her skin. Emily stirred, her eyes fluttering open, and she smiled at me, her dark eyes sparkling with mischief.

"Good morning, Cameron," she purred, her voice still husky from sleep. "Did you sleep well?"

"Better than I ever have," I replied, my voice raspy with emotion. "I can't believe we actually did it."

Emily propped herself up on her elbow, her breast swaying slightly with the movement. "I know. It was amazing. I'm so glad you chose me to be your first, Cameron."

Her words warmed my heart, and I felt a surge of affection for this beautiful woman lying next to me. I wanted to tell her how much she meant to me, but something held me back. Perhaps it was the fear of rejection or the uncertainty of where our relationship was headed. I decided to take a leap of faith and be honest with her.

"Emily, I need to talk to you about last night," I began, my voice steady despite my nerves. "I know we had an agreement, but I can't help the way I feel. I want more than just a physical connection with you."

Emily's eyes widened, and for a moment, I thought I saw a flicker of surprise in them. She sat up, pulling the sheets around her body, her expression turning serious. "Cameron, I appreciate your honesty. I want to be clear about my feelings too. I care about you, and I truly enjoyed our time together. But I think we should stick to our original plan of just being friends."

My heart sank at her words, but I nodded, understanding her perspective. "I get it. I just thought... maybe things could be different between us."

Emily reached out and placed her hand on mine, her touch comforting. "I know, and I'm flattered. But I think it's best if we keep things casual. I don't want to complicate our friendship, and I think this arrangement works for both of us."

I took a deep breath, accepting her decision. "Okay, I can respect that. I just want you to know that I'm here for you, as a friend, and as a... well, a friend with benefits." I couldn't help but smile at the awkwardness of the situation.

Emily laughed, the tension in the room easing. "I'm glad we can be honest with each other. And I do want to see you again, Cameron. I'll be off work at ten, and I'd love to spend some more time with you."

My heart skipped a beat at her suggestion. "I'd like that too. Maybe we can continue where we left off last night?" I asked, my voice dropping to a suggestive tone.

Emily's eyes sparkled with mischief again. "Oh, I think that can be arranged. But for now, let's get some breakfast. I'm starving."

I chuckled, swinging my legs out of bed and reaching for my clothes. "Sounds like a plan. Did you want to go to the boardwalk for some breakfast? My treat?"

"Sounds amazing," she grinned.

After a delicious breakfast of scrambled eggs, pancakes and sausage, Emily and I spent the morning walking the boardwalk, enjoying the ocean breeze and each other's company. We chatted about our lives, our dreams, and the things we loved. I learned more about her family and her passion for helping others, while she listened intently to my tech ventures and my love for comic books. It was easy to forget about the physical aspect of our relationship as we connected on a deeper level.

As the day wore on, the anticipation of our evening plans grew. I couldn't wait to have Emily back in bed, to explore her body and discover new pleasures together.

Later that night, after her shift at work, Emily showed up at my house with an overnight bag to spend the night with me, drinking and having sex. After a couple of rounds of shots of tequila, I suggested we play a game to spice things up.

"How about a game of truth or dare?" I proposed, a mischievous glint in my eye. "It might make things more interesting."

Emily's eyes lit up at the idea. "I love it! Let's do it. Truth or dare?" She asked.

"Truth?" I grinned.

"Tell me your deepest, darkest secret."

I laughed, feeling a bit nervous. "Alright, but you have to promise not to judge me."

"I promise," she said, crossing her heart with her finger.

I took a deep breath, gathering my courage. "My secret is... I have a thing for superhero costumes. I've always wanted to dress up as my favorite character and pretend to be a superhero."

Emily burst into peals of laughter, her eyes sparkling with amusement. "Oh my god, Cameron! That's hilarious! You're such a geek!"

I felt a mix of relief and embarrassment, but mostly I was glad to share this part of myself with Emily. "Well, maybe I'll surprise you with a little costume play later," I teased.

"I can't wait!" she exclaimed, clapping her hands together. "Now, it's my turn."

"Truth or dare?" I asked.

"Truth." She replied.

"What's your favorite sexual position?" I asked.

"I like doggy style. There's nothing like being on all fours with a man, pinning you down, slamming every inch he has into you."

"Sounds hot." I grinned.

"It is, perhaps we can try later."

"I'd like too."

She winked at me and took a deep breath. I loved the way her brown eyes sparkled, turning me on.

"Okay, truth or dare?" She asked.

"Dare," I replied, feeling bold.

Emily's eyes gleamed with mischief. "I dare you to give me a lap dance, right here, right now."

My heart raced as I stood up, feeling a bit self-conscious. But the desire in Emily's eyes urged me on. I put on some music, a slow, sensual track, and began to move my body, letting the rhythm guide me. I slowly approached Emily, who was sitting on the sofa, her eyes locked on me. I ran my hands over my body, teasing her with my movements, then straddled her lap, grinding my hips against her.

Emily's breath quickened, and she reached up to run her hands through my hair, pulling me closer. I leaned in, our lips brushing against each other, and I felt her tongue flick against mine. The kiss deepened, and I could feel her hands roaming over my body, igniting a fire within me.

As the song ended, I pulled away, breathless. "Your turn, Emily. I dare you to do something naughty," I whispered, my voice hoarse with desire.

She bit her lip, a playful glint in her eye. "I have just the thing in mind."

Emily stood up, her movements confident and sensual. She slowly began to undress, revealing her curvy body inch by inch. I watched, mesmerized, as she slid her dress off her shoulders, letting it fall to the floor, leaving her completely naked. Her large, soft breasts swayed with the motion, and her round belly and wide hips were a vision of feminine beauty.

She approached me, her eyes smoldering with desire. "I want to show you something," she whispered, taking my hand and leading me to the bedroom.

In the bedroom, Emily pushed me gently onto the bed, her hands roaming over my chest and abs. I felt her lips trail kisses down my body, her tongue teasing my nipples, sending shivers down my spine. She continued her descent, her mouth leaving a trail of wet kisses along my stomach, until she reached my throbbing erection.

I gasped as she took me into her warm, wet mouth, her tongue swirling around the head of my cock. She looked up at me, her eyes full of lust, as she took me deeper, her hands cupping my balls gently. I moaned, my hands threading through her hair, encouraging her to take more of me.

"Fuck Emily," I breathed.

"You like that papi?" She hummed in response, the vibrations sending me into ecstasy.

"Yes..." I moaned, experiencing my first tantalizing blowjob. I ran my hands along her scalp, holding her in place as she deep-throated me, her skills surpassing my wildest fantasies. I felt my orgasm building, my body tensing with pleasure.

"Emily, I'm gonna cum," I warned, my voice strained.

She pulled off my cock with a pop, her eyes sparkling with satisfaction. "Not yet, papi. I want you to last longer. We're just getting started."

I panted, trying to regain my composure as she climbed on top of me, straddling my waist. She positioned my cock at her entrance, teasing me by rubbing her wetness against the head.

"I want you inside me, Cameron," she whispered, her voice husky with desire. "But first, I want to show you something."

I nodded, my eyes never leaving her gorgeous plus sized body.

Emily reached down, spreading her lips apart, revealing her glistening pussy. "I want you to taste me, baby. I want you to eat me out."

"I've never done that before."

"Don't worry, papi. I'll guide you."

I couldn't believe what I was hearing, but I was more than willing to oblige. I sat up, my mouth watering at the sight of her pink, swollen folds. I leaned in, inhaling her musky scent, then flicked my tongue across her clit, earning a moan from Emily.

"Yes, right there," she whispered, her hands guiding my head.

I dove in, my tongue exploring her folds, tasting her sweetness. I licked and sucked, learning her body, as she writhed above me, her moans growing louder. I loved the way she tasted, the way her body responded to my touch.

"That's it, baby," she encouraged. "Make me cum with your mouth."

I increased my efforts, my tongue working feverishly, my hands squeezing her thighs. Emily's body trembled, her hips bucking against my face as she climaxed, her juices flooding my mouth.

"Oh god, Cameron!" she cried out, her body shaking.

I continued to lap at her sensitive flesh, savoring her flavor, until she gently pushed me away, her breath coming in gasps.

"That was amazing," she whispered, her eyes glistening with pleasure. "Now it's your turn."

I smiled, my body still buzzing with desire. "I can't wait."

Emily reached for a condom on the nightstand, tearing open the packet with her teeth. She rolled it down my length, her touch sending sparks of pleasure through me.

"I like it hard and fast, and doggy style, Cameron," she whispered, positioning herself, in a crotched position with her ass up in the air. "Show me what you've got."

I didn't need any further encouragement. I grabbed her hips, guiding her back onto my cock, filling her in one smooth motion. She gasped, her eyes closing momentarily as she adjusted to my size.

"Fuck, you feel so good," she moaned, beginning to move her hips in a slow, sensual rhythm.

I thrust up to meet her, our bodies moving in perfect sync. I loved the way her big ass bounced off my cock with each stroke, her round cheeks clapping against my thighs. I reached up, squeezing her soft flesh, watching her big ass twerk on my lap, driving me wild.

"That's it, baby," I groaned. "Fuck my cock. Show me how you like it."

Emily's movements became more frantic, her ass cheeks jiggling as she slammed her ass back on my cock, her big ass cheeks bouncing wildly. I reached up, squeezing and pinching her plump flesh, earning a cry of pleasure from her.

"Yes, yes, yes!" she chanted, her body glistening with sweat. "Fuck me harder, Cameron!"

I obliged, my hands gripping her hips tightly, my cock slamming into her with force. I watched, transfixed, as her big ass worked up and down my shaft, her pussy gripping me tightly.

"I'm gonna cum, Emily!" I warned, my body coiled with tension.

"Cum for me, baby," she urged, her nails digging into my chest. "Fill me up."

My release hit me like a freight train, my body convulsing as I emptied my load into the condom, my cock throbbing inside her. Emily collapsed flat on the mattress, her breath coming in pants, her body still quivering from her own orgasm.

When we were done, we laid there, entangled in each other's arms, our hearts racing and our bodies glistening with sweat. I felt a sense of contentment and satisfaction, knowing that this was just the beginning of our sexual journey together.

As we caught our breath, Emily propped herself up on her elbows, her breasts swaying above me. "That was incredible, Cameron. I had no idea you'd be so... passionate."

I grinned, my heart swelling with pride. "I have a lot to learn, but I'm eager to explore more with you. And I think I know just the thing to make it even hotter."

Emily's eyes lit up with curiosity. "Oh yeah? And what's that?"

I winked at her, my mind already spinning with ideas for our next encounter. "You'll just have to wait and see, my sexy friend with benefits. But I promise, it'll be worth the wait."

With that, I pulled her down for a passionate kiss, our lips sealing the promise of more erotic adventures to come.

Chapter 10

The sun-soaked beach day with Emily was a much-needed break from the complexities of my life. I had always been a solitary soul, content with my quiet existence, but today, I embraced the lively energy Emily brought into my world. After our passionate night together, I found myself craving more of her company, not just in the bedroom but also during the day. And what better way to spend a day off than by the ocean?

I watched Emily's curvy figure as she waded through the water, her one-piece bathing suit hugging her body like a second skin. The black fabric accentuated her tan skin, and the way the water clung to her hips and breasts as she emerged from the waves was a sight to behold. Her laughter filled the air as she splashed me, her eyes sparkling with mischief. I couldn't help but join in, splashing her back, feeling like a kid again.

We swam and played like children, reveling in the simple pleasures of the ocean. I dove under the waves, feeling the cool water against my skin, and resurfaced beside her. Emily's face, with her bright smile and sparkling eyes, was a picture of pure joy. I found myself captivated by her, not just physically but by the vibrant spirit she exuded.

As the sun began its descent, we left the water, our skin glistening with saltwater and the warmth of the day. We strolled back to the house, hand in hand, leaving our footprints in the sand. The gentle breeze played with Emily's hair, and she stopped to let it dance in the wind, her eyes closed in contentment.

"I love days like this," she said, turning to me with a radiant smile. "Just you, me, and the ocean. It's like we're the only ones here."

I smiled, nodding in agreement. "It's peaceful. A much-needed break from the chaos."

Emily squeezed my hand. "I'm glad I could be a part of it. I know you like your alone time, but I'm happy to share this with you."

"Same." I grinned. "I haven't felt this good since my before my parent's deaths."

"You don't speak much of them."

"Honestly, I don't like to. They were my everything. My mother taught me how to cook. My father taught me what it was to be a man. They were my world."

"They sound like it."

"That's why I want a family of my own." I admitted.

"Really?"

"Yeah, that's why I bought a house like this. I always envision a big family filling its bedrooms."

"Aww, that's sweet."

"Do you want kids?" I asked.

"I do, but not right now. I came from a poor upbringing, and I don't want the same thing for my children. With the debt that I have it doesn't make sense to bring a child in this world."

"Oh...well, if something would happen between us and we had a kid, I'd be there for you."

"You're too sweet." She smiled, touching my face. "I wish you were my ex who knocked my up when I was eighteen. Perhaps then I would've kept that child."

"You had an abortion?"

She nodded, "I don't like to speak about it. I still feel bad that I made that choice, but honestly, it was the right decision. I was too young for a kid."

I nodded listening to her reasoning.

"I won't be making that mistake again, though. That's why I always have you wear a condom. I'm still not ready for a kid, so until then, the rubber stays on."

"that's fine with me. I like having sex with you, regardless of if a condom is on."

"you're sweet, Cameron, I like having sex with you too."

Her words touched me, and I felt a surge of affection for this vibrant woman. I stopped walking and turned to face her, taking in her beauty—the wind-tousled hair, the freckles on her nose, and the mischievous glint in her eyes.

"You know, Emily, I've never been much of a social butterfly. I prefer my solitude, but with you, it's different. I find myself wanting to share these moments."

Emily's smile softened, and she stepped closer, her curvy body pressing against mine. "I know, Cameron. I feel the same. You're not like anyone I've ever met. You're kind, sweet, and so damn sexy." Her fingers traced the outline of my jaw, sending shivers down my spine.

I leaned in, capturing her lips in a tender kiss. The taste of salt and sun on her lips was intoxicating. Our kiss deepened, fueled by the passion that had been building between us. My hands found their way to her hips, pulling her closer, feeling the softness of her body against mine.

Breaking away, I took her hand and led her back to the house, the anticipation of the evening ahead lingering in the air. As we showered together, washing away the sand and saltwater, our hands roamed freely, exploring each other's bodies. The warm water cascaded over us, turning our skin into a canvas of desire. I lathered her hair, massaging her scalp, and kissed her neck, making her moan softly.

"I love how you touch me, Cameron," she whispered, her breath hot against my ear. "It's like you know exactly what I need."

I smiled, my hands sliding down her back, cupping her full buttocks. "I want to make you feel good, Emily. I want to give you everything."

I slipped a finger inside her velvet hole, and she collapsed on me moaning.

"Just like that, papi..." her hand reached down and tugged at my hard cock, making me groan.

"Fuck..." I hissed.

"Take a breath, papi. Save it for later." She whispered seductively in my ear making me shiver. "Let's get out and enjoy the rest of the night before we fuck."

"Okay." I grinned.

The shower became a steamy prelude to what was yet to come, and I couldn't wait to feel her curves on my cock again. We toweled off, our bodies still flushed with desire, and I led her to my bedroom, the master suite with its luxurious amenities. The setting sun painted the sky in hues of orange and pink, creating a romantic ambiance.

I opened the sliding glass door, leading to the patio, where the fire pit glowed, casting a warm glow on the outdoor seating area. The sound of the waves crashing in the distance provided a soothing backdrop to our evening.

"I thought we could have dinner out here," I said, my heart racing with anticipation. "Just the two of us under the stars."

Emily's eyes sparkled with delight. "That sounds perfect, papi. I love being spoiled by you."

I prepared a simple yet delicious meal, grilling fresh mahi-mahi and whipping up a homemade mango salsa. The sweet and spicy flavors complemented the fish perfectly. We sat on the plush outdoor sofa, our legs intertwined and sipped on sangria as the sky transitioned from dusk to night. The moon, a slender crescent, hung low in the sky, casting a silvery light over the ocean.

"This is so romantic, Cameron," Emily purred, leaning into me. "I feel like we're the only ones in the world."

I kissed her temple, inhaling the scent of her hair, a mix of saltwater and coconut from her shampoo. "I want to make every moment special with you, Emily. I want to show you how much I care."

As the sangria loosened our inhibitions, our hands began to wander, exploring each other's bodies with a newfound urgency. Emily's fingers traced the waistband of my shorts, and I felt my desire for her intensify.

"I want you, Cameron," she whispered, her breath hot against my neck. "I want to feel you inside me, right here, under the stars."

Her words sent a bolt of desire through me, and I couldn't resist her any longer. I stood, taking her hand, and led her to the soft sand, where the waves lapped gently at the shore. The moonlight illuminated her beautiful face, her eyes sparkling with anticipation.

I kissed her, my hands eagerly tugging at her sundress, revealing her voluptuous curves. Her breasts, full and heavy, spilled out of her dress, and I couldn't help but admire them. My hands cupped their softness, my thumbs brushing over her nipples, now hardened with desire.

"You're so beautiful, Emily," I breathed, my voice hoarse with want. "I want to worship every inch of you."

She moaned as I kissed my way down her body, my lips trailing over her sensitive skin. I unclasped her bra, freeing her breasts, and took one nipple into my mouth, suckling gently. She arched her back, pressing her chest into my face, encouraging my attentions.

"Oh, Cameron, yes," she panted, her hands threading through my hair. "Your mouth feels so good."

I paid homage to her body, my lips and tongue exploring every inch of her soft skin. I kissed her neck, her shoulders, and the curve of her waist, leaving a trail of kisses down to the moist heat between her thighs.

"Please, Cameron," she begged, her voice thick with need. "I need you now."

I reached for the condom in my pocket, quickly sheathing myself, and positioned myself between her legs. I looked into her eyes, seeing the desire and trust reflected there, and slowly entered her.

Emily gasped as I filled her, her body welcoming mine. I paused, letting her adjust to my size, before beginning a slow, rhythmic thrust. The sound of the ocean provided a sensual soundtrack to our lovemaking, and the sand beneath us added a wild, untamed element to the encounter.

I held her hips, guiding our movements, as our passion intensified. Emily's hands gripped my shoulders, her nails digging into my skin, leaving marks of passion. Her breasts swayed with each thrust, and I leaned down to capture a nipple in my mouth, sucking gently as I continued to drive into her.

"Oh, yes, Cameron," she cried out, her voice hoarse and raw. "Fuck me harder, papi. Make me cum."

Her words spurred me on, and I complied, picking up the pace. My hands grasped her curvy hips, holding her firmly as I plunged into her with abandon. The sight of her breasts bouncing with each thrust was incredibly arousing, and I couldn't hold back any longer.

"I'm close, Emily," I groaned, my voice strained. "I'm gonna cum."

"Yes, papi, fill me," she urged, her nails digging deeper into my flesh. "Cum with me."

Our orgasms crashed over us like waves, washing away any inhibitions. I thrust into her one final time, my body shuddering as I released myself, and felt Emily's muscles clench around me, milking my cock. We cried out in unison, our voices mingling with the sound of the ocean, a primal chorus of pleasure.

As our breathing slowed, I collapsed onto the sand beside her, my body spent but satisfied. Emily turned to me, her eyes sparkling with afterglow, and kissed me softly.

"That was incredible, Cameron," she whispered, her fingers tracing my jawline. "I've never done it on the beach before. It was wild and passionate."

I smiled, my heart full. "I'm glad I could give you that experience. I want to give you everything, Emily. I want to make you happy."

She snuggled closer, her curvy body fitting perfectly against mine. "You already do, Cameron. You're so sweet and caring. I feel like I can be myself with you."

We lay there for a while, listening to the ocean and the distant sounds of the nightlife. The night was young, and I knew there were more adventures to be had, more experiences to share with this incredible woman. But for now, I was content to lie here, under the stars, with Emily in my arms, savoring the moment.

Little did I know that our journey together was about to take an unexpected turn, one that would challenge and change us both in ways we never could have imagined.

Chapter 11

I couldn't wait to hear from Emily again, and when my phone lit up with her name flashing on the screen, my heart skipped a beat. I answered with a mix of excitement and nervousness, my palms already beginning with a light sweat.

"Hey, Cameron, it's Emily. How are you doing?" Her voice was like warm honey, smooth and inviting. I could almost feel her breath on my neck, sending shivers down my spine.

"I'm good, I'm good. Just getting some work done. How about you? Everything okay?" I tried to keep my tone casual, but my heart was racing. The last time we spoke, we had made plans for a steamy evening, but life had gotten in the way.

"I'm doing great, papi. I was wondering if we could pick up where we left off. You know, finish what we started," she purred, and I could picture her biting her full lower lip, a mischievous glint in her dark eyes.

I cleared my throat, suddenly feeling a little nervous. "Well, I'm not sure about tonight. I actually have plans to go to this comic con in Las Vegas. It's a big deal for me." I explained, a hint of disappointment creeping into my voice.

"Oh, a comic con! That sounds like so much fun! I've always wanted to go to one of those. Could it be possible if I come along?" Her enthusiasm was infectious, and I found myself smiling at the idea of having her by my side.

"Of course, you're more than welcome to join me. I mean, it's not every day that you get to attend one of the biggest comic cons in the world. And I'd love to show you around geek culture." I couldn't help but laugh at the thought of poshy Emily in my geeky paradise, her vibrant energy contrasting with the nerdy atmosphere.

"Really? You're not just saying that because you feel bad for me?" She teased, her voice playful.

"No, I promise. It'll be fun. And what's the point of having all this money if I can't spoil my friends a little, right?" I joked, thinking of the lavish hotel suite I had booked for the trip.

Emily giggled, a sound that always made my stomach flutter. "You're such a sweet talker, Cameron. I can't say no to you. I'll start packing right away. And who knows, maybe I'll even dress up as a superheroine!"

As we hung up, I felt a surge of excitement. Emily was spontaneous, and her willingness to embrace my interests made my heart swell. I knew I had to make this trip memorable, not just for the comic con but for the potential adventure with Emily.

***

The flight to Las Vegas was uneventful, but Emily's presence made it feel like a thrilling journey. She sat beside me, her curvy body pressed against mine, and I couldn't help but steal glances at her. She wore a loose-fitting dress, her dark hair cascading over her shoulders, and her full lips were painted a bright red. She noticed me looking and winked, her eyes sparkling with mischief.

"You're staring, Cameron. Is it my superpower to make you blush?" She teased, her hand reaching over to squeeze my thigh.

I felt my cheeks warm, but I didn't look away. "Maybe it is. I like the idea of you having secret powers, especially if they involve making me feel this way." I whispered, leaning closer.

She grinned, her breath brushing my lips. "Oh, I have many powers, and I plan to show them all to you. But first, let's enjoy the con. I want to see what all the fuss is about."

As we landed in Las Vegas, the city welcomed us with its dazzling lights and vibrant energy. I had booked a luxurious hotel suite, complete with a breathtaking view of the Strip. Emily's eyes widened as we entered the room, taking in the spacious living area and the floor-to-ceiling windows.

"This is incredible, Cameron! You really know how to treat a girl." She exclaimed, dropping her bag and running to the window, her eyes sparkling with delight.

I smiled, feeling a rush of satisfaction. "I wanted to make this trip special. And I thought, what better way than to have a superhero-themed adventure?"

"Oh, I love it! Let's dress up and get into character!" Emily's enthusiasm was contagious, and soon we were rummaging through our bags, pulling out costumes we had hastily packed.

I chose a classic superhero outfit, complete with a red cape and a muscular chest piece. I slipped into the blue bodysuit, feeling a bit self-conscious about my skinny frame, but Emily's presence boosted my confidence. She transformed into a sexy version of a super woman hero, her curvy body accentuated by the tight red and gold corset and the short blue skirt. Her tanned thick thighs were encased in tall red boots, and she had a golden tiara perched on her dark waves.

"Damn, you look incredible," I breathed, my eyes tracing the curves of her body.

Emily struck a playful pose with one hand on her hip. "I'm here to save the day. And I think we should start by saving each other from our inhibitions."

I felt my dick stirring in my tight spandex, and I adjusted myself, trying to maintain my composure. "I'm all for that. But first, let's explore the con. I want to show you why I love this world so much."

Hand in hand, we ventured into the bustling convention center, our costumes attracting attention and smiles. Emily was a natural, striking poses and interacting with other cosplayers. I felt a sense of pride as I watched her embrace the geeky culture, her laughter ringing through the halls.

We spent hours wandering the exhibit halls, meeting artists, and immersing ourselves in the fantasy world. Emily was fascinated by the intricate details of the comic book art, and her curiosity knew no bounds. We even participated in a superhero-themed game show, where our knowledge of comic lore was put to the test. Our playful rivalry kept the audience entertained, and we ended up winning a signed comic book each.

As the day turned to evening, we found ourselves in a dimly lit hotel bar, still wearing our costumes from the con. The air was still buzzing with excitement from our day. We've had a couple of drinks and naturally our judgment wasn't where it should be. I was as drunk as she was as her eyes sparkled with a mischievous gleam. Fuck me, did she look sexy in her low-cut costume as she leaned across the table, her generous cleavage on full display.

"So, I have a confession. I've been a naughty girl today. I forgot to pack any condoms," she whispered, her voice low and sultry.

My heart raced, and I felt a familiar stirring in my groin. "Oh? And what does that mean for us?" I asked, playing along with her sexy role-play.

"It means, my dear superhero, that we have two options. We can either call it a night and wait for another time, or..." She trailed off, her eyes locking with mine, daring me to fill in the blank.

"Or we can be spontaneous and embrace the moment. After all, superheroes are known for their quick thinking and bravery, right?" I suggested, my voice hoarse with desire.

Emily's full lips curved into a seductive smile. "Exactly. And I think we should use our superpowers to make this night unforgettable."

Without another word, she stood, her movements graceful and deliberate. She walked around the table, her hips swaying, and took my hand, leading me out of the bar. We made our way back to the hotel suite, our footsteps quickening with anticipation.

The moment we entered the room, Emily turned to me, her eyes burning with passion. She pressed me against the wall, her soft body molding to mine. I groaned, feeling her firm breasts against my chest, and my hands instinctively went to her hips, pulling her closer.

"I want you, Cameron. I want to feel you inside me, filling me up," she whispered, her breath hot against my ear.

I couldn't resist her any longer. My hands roamed over her body, tracing the curves of her waist, her soft stomach, and finally cupping her full breasts. I teased her nipples through the corset, enjoying the way she arched into my touch.

"Emily, you drive me crazy," I murmured, my lips finding her neck, kissing and sucking gently.

She moaned, her hands working on the zipper of my bodysuit. "I want to feel your skin against mine. Let's get out of these costumes."

With eager fingers, we undressed each other, our movements hurried and passionate. Her corset was unlaced, revealing her heavy breasts, the nipples already hard and begging for attention. I lowered my head, taking one taut peak into my mouth, and suckled gently, then harder as she began to writhe and moan.

"Oh, yes, Cameron, that feels so good. Suck my tits, papi," she panted, her hands threading through my hair, urging me on.

I obliged, lavishing attention on her luscious breasts, while my hands traveled lower, exploring the soft skin of her belly and the curve of her hips. My fingers found the waistband of her tiny skirt, and I slowly peeled it down her thighs, revealing a pair of sheer panties, already damp with her arousal.

"Mmm, someone's ready for me," I whispered, my voice husky with desire.

Emily giggled, a sultry sound that sent a shiver down my spine. "I'm always ready for you, Superman. But tonight, I want to be Wonder Woman. I want to ride you, hard and fast."

She pushed me towards the bed, and I fell back, my eyes never leaving her as she stepped out of her skirt and kicked off her boots. She stood before me, clad only in her panties and tiara, a vision of sensuality and power.

I reached out, sliding my hands up her thighs, reveling in the softness of her skin. I hooked my fingers into the sides of her panties and slowly slid them down, revealing her glistening pussy lips.

"Damn, you're beautiful," I breathed, my eyes feasting on the sight of her.

Emily smiled, a wicked gleam in her eyes. She climbed onto the bed, straddling my hips, and positioned herself over my throbbing erection. I felt the heat of her pussy, the dampness of her arousal, as she slowly lowered herself onto me.

"Oh, fuck, that feels so good," she moaned, her eyes closing in ecstasy.

I groaned, my hands gripping her hips, helping her set a slow, torturous rhythm. I watched, transfixed, as her full breasts bounced with each downward thrust, her nipples hard and pointing at the ceiling.

"You like the view, Mr. Superhero?" She teased, her voice breathless.

"I love it," I managed to reply, my body on fire. "But I want to see more. I want to watch you come."

Emily smiled, a devilish glint in her eyes. "Then watch closely, papi."

She began to move faster, her hips rolling and grinding against me. Her hands reached up, tugging at her tiara, and she tossed it aside, her dark hair falling around her shoulders. She threw her head back, her large saggy breasts jiggling, and I knew she was close.

"Oh, fuck, I'm gonna come, Cameron! Keep fucking me, papi!" She cried out, her body trembling.

I held her hips, my hands leaving red marks on her soft skin, and drove into her with all the force I could muster. Her pussy clenched around me, rippling and pulsing, and she cried out, her orgasm washing over her in waves.

"Yes, yes, YES!" She screamed, her body bucking wildly, her juices flowing freely, coating my cock and balls.

I held her, my own orgasm building to a crescendo. I felt her pussy milking my shaft, and with a final, powerful thrust, I came, filling her with my seed.

We collapsed onto the bed, our hearts racing, our bodies slick with sweat and the evidence of our passion. Emily turned to me, her eyes sparkling with satisfaction.

"That was incredible, Cameron. I never knew superhero sex could be so hot," she purred, her fingers tracing lazy circles on my chest.

I smiled, feeling a deep sense of contentment. "It's all about embracing your powers, Mrs.Hero. And I think we've only just begun to discover our true potential."

As we lay there, sated and exhausted, I knew that this trip to Las Vegas had been about more than just the comic con. It was the beginning of a new chapter in our relationship, one filled with adventure, passion, and the boundless possibilities of two people exploring their desires.

And as we drifted off to sleep, I couldn't help but wonder what other sexy surprises this convention had in store for us.

Chapter 12

I woke up with a throbbing headache, the sunlight streaming through the hotel room window piercing my eyes. I groaned and rolled over, reaching for my phone on the bedside table. As I checked the time, I realized it was already past noon. The events of the previous night came flooding back to me, and I couldn't help but smile. Emily and I had truly let loose at the comic con, dressing up as our favorite superheroes and immersing ourselves in the geeky paradise.

"Good morning, sleepyhead," Emily's voice startled me as she appeared in the doorway, a mischievous smile on her face. "Or should I say, good afternoon?"

I rubbed my eyes and sat up, noticing Emily's superhero costume still clinging to her curves. "Hey, good morning to you too. How are you feeling?" I asked, concerned about her well-being after our wild night.

Emily laughed, shaking her head. "I'm feeling a little hungover, to be honest. But it was worth it! Last night was amazing, Cameron. I mean, who would've thought we'd end up..." She trailed off, her cheeks flushing with embarrassment.

"Yeah, I know. I can't believe we did it in costume," I admitted, feeling a mix of satisfaction and unease. "How much did we drink anyway?"

Emily shrugged, her eyes sparkling with mischief. "Enough to make some questionable decisions, I guess. But it was fun, right?"

"Definitely fun," I agreed, recalling the intense passion we had shared. I suddenly remembered something crucial, and my heart sank. "Wait, did we... I mean, did we use protection?"

Emily's face fell, and she buried her hands in her hair. "Oh no, I completely forgot about that. I'm so sorry, Cameron. I don't know what I was thinking. We were both caught up in the moment."

"It's okay, Emily. It's not your fault. We were both drunk and..." I paused, not wanting to make her feel worse.

"It's fine, really. It was a one-time thing, and we were responsible enough to get tested before. But still, I should've been more careful," she said, her voice filled with regret.

I swung my legs out of bed and walked over to her, taking her hands in mine. "Hey, it's okay. We're both adults, and these things happen. I'm just glad we're on the same page about this being a one-time thing."

Emily looked into my eyes, her expression softening. "I am too. I mean, we've always kept our relationship casual, right? It's just... I didn't expect last night to be so..."

"Incredible?" I suggested, my heart racing at the memory of her riding me with such fervor.

"Exactly. But it's fine, we can move past this. Let's just enjoy the rest of the convention and forget about last night's... mishap," she said, squeezing my hands.

I nodded, feeling a sense of relief. "Sounds like a plan. Let's get some breakfast and explore the convention some more. There are still plenty of panels and events to check out."

As we made our way out of the hotel room, hand in hand, I couldn't help but feel a sense of excitement for the day ahead. The comic con was bustling with activity, and we spent the next few hours wandering through the exhibit hall, taking photos with cosplayers, and browsing the various stalls.

We were admiring a life-size replica of the superhero when I heard a familiar voice calling my name. I turned around and my heart skipped a beat as I saw Abby, her blonde hair shining in the convention center's lights. She looked stunning in a vintage comic book t-shirt and jeans, her glasses reflecting the excitement in her eyes.

"Cameron! I can't believe it's you!" Abby exclaimed, rushing over to me and giving me a warm hug. "What are you doing here?"

I smiled, feeling a rush of emotions as I caught a whiff of her familiar scent. "Abby, it's great to see you too. I'm here with... a friend. We're having a blast at the convention." I glanced at Emily, who was standing a few feet away, her expression unreadable.

Abby followed my gaze, and her smile faltered slightly. "Oh, hi! Emily, nice to see you again." She waved towards Emily.

"It's Abby, right?" she replied, her voice colder than usual. "I'm Cameron's... friend."

"Oh, I know Cameron told me all about you! I'm glad y'all made up." Abby winked.

I could sense the tension between the two women, and I quickly jumped in to ease the awkwardness. "Abby, it's been a while. How have you been? I heard you were working on a big project in Los Angeles."

Abby's face lit up as she started telling me about her recent work on a blockbuster movie, her passion for visual effects evident in her animated gestures. "It's been intense, but I'm almost done. I'm actually heading back to Virginia Beach soon. I'd love to catch up properly, Cameron. Maybe we can grab a drink or dinner?"

"Definitely," I replied, my heart racing at the prospect of spending more time with Abby. I had missed her terribly after our abrupt goodbye at the Renaissance Festival.

As we exchanged contact details, I noticed Emily's eyes narrowing slightly, her jaw clenching. I turned to her, sensing her unease. "Is everything okay, Emily? Do you want to grab some lunch? We can find a quiet spot away from the crowds."

Emily shook her head, her expression hardening. "No, I'm fine. I think I'll just head back to the hotel and rest for a bit. You two go ahead and catch up. I'll see you later, Cameron." With that, she turned and walked away, her shoulders hunched and her stride purposeful.

I was confused by her sudden departure, but Abby's presence distracted me from my concerns. "Wow, she seems a bit upset. Is everything okay between you two?"

I sighed, running a hand through my hair. "To be honest, I'm not sure. Emily and I have a complicated relationship. We started as friends with benefits, but lately, it's been more than just casual."

Abby's eyes widened, and she placed a comforting hand on my arm. "I see. It's always tricky when feelings get involved. Maybe she's just feeling a bit insecure with me around. I mean, we did have a pretty intense connection, didn't we?"

"Yeah, we did," I agreed, remembering the fiery passion Abby and I had shared. "But with Emily, it's different. She's been helping me come out of my shell, teaching me how to be more confident and social. I really care about her, but I'm not sure where we stand."

Abby smiled, her eyes filled with understanding. "It sounds like you have some important conversations ahead of you, Cameron. Just remember to be honest with yourself and with her. Follow your heart, and everything will work out."

I nodded, grateful for her advice. "Thanks, Abby. I think I need to have a serious talk with Emily when we get back. In the meantime, let's enjoy the rest of the convention. There's a panel on indie comic artists starting soon that I think you'll love."

As we made our way towards the panel room, I knew I needed to address the growing tension between Emily and me. While I had strong feelings for Abby, something else pulled me to Emily too.

Chapter 13

I arrived back at the hotel room, exhausted but content after a fun day at Comic-Con with Abby. It had been an enjoyable experience, and I was looking forward to some rest. But as I unlocked the door and stepped inside, I was met with a sight that instantly jolted me out of my post-convention buzz. Emily was sitting on the bed, her face buried in her hands, shoulders shaking. Hearing the door open, she quickly wiped her tears and tried to compose herself, but I could still see the redness in her eyes.

"Hey, Em," I said softly, closing the door behind me. "What's wrong?"

She sniffled and shot me a look that was a mix of anger and sadness. "Did you have a good time with her?" she asked, her voice laced with emotion.

I was taken aback by her question and the underlying accusation in her tone. "What? With Abby? Yeah, it was fun. Why? Are you okay?"

Emily's eyes narrowed, and she let out a frustrated sigh. "Don't play dumb, Cameron. You know why I'm upset."

I racked my brain, trying to figure out what could have possibly upset her. Had I said something insensitive? Or was this about something else entirely? I decided to take a chance and be direct. "Emily, please, talk to me. You're not making sense."

She glared at me, her eyes glistening with fresh tears. "You really don't get it, do you? I thought you were different, but I guess I was wrong."

My heart sank as I realized this was about more than just a bad day. "Emily, I'm sorry. I don't want to fight. Can you just tell me what's bothering you?"

She took a deep breath, as if gathering her courage. "Fine, I'll tell you. I like you, okay? I've had feelings for you for a while now."

Her confession caught me off guard, and I felt my face grow warm. I had always thought of Emily as a friend, a close one at that, but I never imagined she saw me as more. I struggled to find the right words, not wanting to hurt her. "Emily, I... I had no idea. I thought we were just friends."

"Yeah, that's what I thought too," she said, her voice cracking. "But I can't deny how I feel anymore. Seeing you with Abby today, it just hit me. I can't stand the thought of you with someone else."

I took a step closer to her, my heart racing. "Emily, I... I don't know what to say. I care about you, but I never wanted to cross that line."

She looked up at me, her eyes pleading. "It's okay if you choose her, Cameron. I get it. You have so much in common, and you'd make a great couple. I just wanted you to know how I feel."

I shook my head, my mind racing. "No, Emily. It's not like that. I care about Abby, but it's different with you. You've been there for me when no one else was. You're special to me."

Her eyes widened, and a glimmer of hope appeared in her tear-stained face. "What do you mean?"

I took a deep breath, my heart pounding in my chest. "I mean, I want to be with you, Emily. I want you to be my girlfriend."

A wide smile spread across her face, and she threw her arms around me, pulling me into a tight embrace. "Really? You mean it?"

I returned her hug, feeling a surge of happiness. "Of course, I mean it. I want to be with you, and only you."

Emily pulled back, her eyes sparkling with joy. "Oh, Cameron, I've wanted this for so long. I thought you'd never see me as more than a friend."

I caressed her cheek, feeling a sense of wonder at how our relationship had evolved. "I'm sorry I was so blind. But I'm not letting you go now that I've found you."

She giggled, her cheeks flushing. "You're such a dork, but I love it. I love you, Cameron Briggs."

I grinned, feeling like the luckiest guy in the world. "I love you too, Emily Lopez. And I can't wait to show you just how much."

As our lips met in a passionate kiss, all the pent-up emotions of the day seemed to melt away. Emily's lips were soft and warm, and she tasted like the sweetest candy. I wrapped my arms around her, pulling her closer, and she responded eagerly, her hands running through my hair.

Our kiss deepened, and I could feel her body pressing against mine, her curves molding perfectly to my frame. My hands roamed over her back, feeling the softness of her skin beneath her dress. I wanted to touch every inch of her, to explore the body that had haunted my dreams for so long.

Breaking away from the kiss, Emily looked up at me, her eyes sparkling with desire. "I want you, Cameron. Right here, right now."

I didn't need any further encouragement. I grabbed her hand and led her to the bed, my heart pounding with anticipation. I gently pushed her down onto the mattress, and she giggled, her eyes filled with mischief.

"You're so cute when you're all serious," she teased, reaching up to stroke my cheek.

I couldn't help but smile, feeling a surge of affection for this amazing woman. "I'm serious about making you feel good, Emily. Very serious."

She bit her lip, her eyes fluttering shut as I leaned down to kiss her again. This time, I took my time, exploring her mouth with my tongue, savoring the taste of her. I could feel her body responding, her breath quickening as I trailed kisses down her neck, nipping at her sensitive skin.

Emily moaned softly, her hands gripping my shoulders, urging me on. I wanted to take my time, to savor every moment, but my body had other ideas. I was already rock hard, my cock straining against my jeans, desperate to be freed.

With trembling fingers, I reached for the button of my jeans, undoing them and pushing them down my hips. Emily's eyes widened as my erection sprang free, thick and eager.

"Oh my," she breathed, her eyes fixed on my cock. "You're so big, Cameron. I can't wait to feel you inside me."

Her words sent a jolt of desire through me, and I couldn't wait any longer. After grabbing a condom from my suitcase, I climbed onto the bed, positioning myself between her legs, my cock brushing against her soft inner thighs.

"Are you ready for me, Emily?" I asked, my voice hoarse with desire.

She nodded; her eyes locked on mine. "I've been ready for you since the moment I met you, Cameron. Take me, please."

I unraveled the condom and placed it on. Once my hard cock was sheathed by the latex, I positioned myself at her entrance, feeling the warmth of her wetness as I teased her with the tip of my cock. She was so tight, and I wanted to make this moment last. But my body had other ideas, and with a powerful thrust, I sank deep into her, filling her completely.

Emily gasped, her back arching off the bed as she adjusted to my size. "Oh god, you feel amazing," she moaned, her hands gripping my hips.

I held still, reveling in the sensation of being inside her, wanting to give her time to adjust. But she had other plans, and with a hungry look in her eyes, she urged me on.

"Move, Cameron. Please, I need more," she pleaded, her voice thick with desire.

I began to move, slowly at first, sliding in and out of her tight heat. With each thrust, I went a little deeper, a little harder, until I was pounding into her, our bodies slapping together in a frenzied rhythm.

Emily's moans filled the room, her nails digging into my back as she met my thrusts, her body moving in perfect harmony with mine.

I could feel her muscles clenching around my cock, milking me, and I knew I wouldn't last much longer.

"Oh, Emily, I'm so close," I groaned, my voice ragged as I pounded into her.

"Yes, Cameron, come for me," she panted, her eyes wild with passion. "Fill me up, papi."

Her words were my undoing, and with a final, powerful thrust, I exploded inside her, my cock pulsing as I filled the condom with my hot cum. Emily cried out, her body convulsing around me as she came, her orgasm rippling through her.

After tossing the filled condom in the trash, I laid back down with her. In the bed, we lay there, entangled in each other's arms, our hearts pounding and our bodies slick with sweat. I kissed her forehead, my chest heaving as I tried to catch my breath.

"That was incredible, Emily," I whispered, my voice hoarse. "I've never felt anything like that before."

She smiled, her eyes sparkling with satisfaction. "I know, papi. I felt it too. That was the best orgasm I've ever had."

I grinned, feeling a sense of pride and accomplishment. "I'm glad I could give you that, my love. But we're not done yet. I want to make you feel even better."

Her eyes widened with curiosity and anticipation. "Oh yeah? What do you have in mind, Cameron?"

I winked at her, my mind already racing with ideas. "You'll see, my sexy girlfriend. But first, I need to taste you. I want to make you come with my mouth."

Emily's breath caught in her throat, and she bit her lip, her eyes filled with desire. "Oh, Cameron, you're so naughty. I can't wait to see what you have planned."

I kissed her softly, my hands roaming over her body, exploring her curves as I moved down her body. I wanted to savor every inch of her, to worship her with my mouth and fingers.

Reaching her thighs, I gently parted her legs, revealing her glistening pussy, already swollen and wet from our passionate lovemaking. I inhaled her scent, a heady mix of sex and desire, and I couldn't wait to taste her.

I leaned in, my tongue flicking out to tease her clit, sending shivers through her body. Emily moaned, her hands gripping the sheets as I licked and sucked at her sensitive bud, driving her wild.

"Oh, Cameron, yes," she panted, her hips thrusting up to meet my mouth. "That feels so good, papi. Don't stop."

I smiled against her wetness, my fingers sliding into her, curling and stroking as I sucked and licked her clit, driving her closer to the edge. Emily's moans grew louder, her body tensing as she neared her climax.

"Oh god, I'm gonna come, Cameron," she cried out, her back arching off the bed.

I increased the pressure, my tongue flicking faster, my fingers working in perfect rhythm as I devoured her sweet pussy. Emily's body convulsed, her orgasm ripping through her as she cried out my name, her juices flooding my mouth.

I continued to lick and suck, milking her orgasm, until her body finally relaxed, trembling and spent. I kissed her inner thighs, my face glistening with her essence, and then looked up at her, my eyes filled with adoration.

"That was amazing, Emily," I whispered, my voice hoarse with desire. "But I'm not done with you yet. I want to make you come again, and again."

She smiled; her eyes heavy with lust. "Oh, Cameron, you're insatiable. But I love it. I can't wait to see what else you have in store for me."

I grinned, my mind already spinning with ideas for our next round of passionate lovemaking. But first, I wanted to savor the moment, to hold her close and let her know just how much she meant to me.

"I love you, Emily Lopez," I whispered, my arms wrapped tightly around her. "And I can't wait to show you just how much."

She snuggled into my embrace, her fingers tracing patterns on my back. "I love you too, Cameron Briggs. And I can't wait to see what the future holds for us."

As we lay there, content in each other's arms, I knew that this was just the beginning of our journey together. And I couldn't wait to see where our love would take us next.

Chapter 14

The previous night had been magical. Emily and I had stayed up late, laughing and talking, sharing our dreams and desires. We had connected on a deeper level, and I knew then that I wanted her in my life, not just as my dating coach but as my partner.

Honestly, I couldn't be happier that I was with Emily. I loved looking at her nude tan curves poking from the covers. My cock twitched imaging being buried in her curves yet again. I smiled realizing that she was mine. She was all fucking mine. I gently kissed her cheek, and she stirred in bed still sleeping. I gently brushed some hair from her face and got out of bed. I knew I had to tell Abby about Emily and me. Hopefully she would be okay with it. After putting on some sweatpants, I left the bedroom to dial Abby's number. As the phone rang, my heart raced as I prepared to tell her about my decision.

"Hey, Abby," I said, my voice steady despite the butterflies in my stomach. "I wanted to let you know that Emily and I are officially dating now." There was a brief silence on the other end, and I could almost see Abby's surprised expression. She had been a good friend and a potential love interest, but my heart had chosen Emily.

"Oh, Cameron, that's wonderful!" Abby's voice was warm and sincere. "I'm so happy for you. She's a great girl, and you two make a perfect couple." Her words were like a balm to my soul, easing the guilt I felt for choosing Emily over her. I knew Abby deserved someone who could love her wholeheartedly, and I wasn't ready for that commitment.

"Thank you, Abby," I replied, feeling a weight lift from my shoulders. "I really appreciate your support. You've been a great friend, and I hope we can still hang out sometime."

"Of course, Cameron. I'd love that. And remember, if you ever need to talk or need any advice, I'm just a call away." Her kindness touched me, and I realized how lucky I was to have such understanding people in my life.

As I hung up the phone, a wide smile spread across my face. I felt liberated, like a weight had been lifted from my shoulders. Now, I could fully embrace my relationship with Emily without any reservations. I decided to make our last night in Las Vegas one to remember.

I walked back into the bedroom and laid next to Emily. I gently massaged her shoulder and whispered in her ear. "Hey, gorgeous, I have a surprise for our last night in Vegas. We are going to get dressed up and pretend we're high rollers for the evening."

Emily stirred in bed, and she turned to smile at me. "Oh, Cameron, you're such a romantic nerd! I love it! What do you have in mind?"

"You'll see," I teased, my heart fluttering with anticipation. "Let's something to eat and then go shopping. I want you to wear a sexy low-cut dress."

"And want are you going to wear?"

"you'd see..." I grinned.

As the sun set over the glittering city of Las Vegas, I stood in our hotel suite's living room, admiring my reflection in the mirror. I had donned a sleek tuxedo, the black fabric hugging my tall, skinny frame. My black-rimmed glasses added a touch of sophistication to my nerdy persona. I felt like a different man, exuding confidence and charm, ready to sweep Emily off her feet.

The bedroom door opened, and Emily stood in the doorway, taking my breath away. She looked stunning in a deep red, figure-hugging dress that accentuated her curvy figure. Her light tanned skin glowed under the soft lighting, and her brunette hair fell in soft waves around her shoulders. Her bright smile and sparkling eyes told me she was pleased with my surprise.

"Wow, Cameron, you clean up nice!" She purred, running her hands appreciatively over my tux. "I feel like I'm dating a millionaire tonight."

I chuckled, taking her hand in mine. "I am a millionaire, but that's not the point. You're the million-dollar prize, Emily. Tonight, we're going to live like high rollers and make memories we'll never forget."

We stepped out into the vibrant Las Vegas night, the city's energy buzzing around us. I guided Emily to a luxurious casino, the sound of slot machines and laughter filling the air. I wanted to show her a side of me she had never experienced before, a side that wasn't geeky and nerdy. I wanted to have fun with her. I wanted to give her world of glitz and glamour. I wanted to show her that she was my world.

As we entered the casino, heads turned, and eyes followed us. I felt like a king with my beautiful queen by my side. We sat at a high-stakes table, and I placed a substantial bet, my heart pounding with excitement. The croupier spun the roulette wheel, and the ball bounced and landed on my number.

"Winner!" the croupier announced, and the crowd around us erupted in cheers. Emily squealed with delight, throwing her arms around me. I felt like the luckiest man alive as I collected our winnings, a substantial pile of chips.

"I can't believe it, Cameron!" Emily exclaimed, her eyes sparkling with excitement. "We're on a winning streak! Let's keep playing!"

We spent the next hour gambling, our luck holding strong. With each win, we grew more daring, placing larger bets and relishing the thrill of victory. The pile of chips in front of us grew, and so did our excitement.

"I think it's time to cash in our chips, baby," I suggested, my voice husky with desire. "But first, I have another surprise for you."

Emily's eyes widened with anticipation as I led her to a private room in the casino, a secluded space that I rented from the casino with couches and a dimly lit pole in the center. Soft music played in the background, setting the mood.

"Is this the surprise?" She asked looking around the private room.

"Yeah, the casino comp me the place. It's just us in here. No cameras."

"Really..." a naughty look caught her eye as she smiled and looked at the stripper pole in the room.

Reading her mind, I nodded and looked at the pole.

"Go on, Emily," I urged, my voice thick with desire. "Show me what you've got."

Emily's eyes smoldered as she approached the pole, her hips swaying seductively. She placed her hands on the cool metal, her fingers gripping tightly as she began to move. Her body undulated, her curves swaying in perfect rhythm to the music. I was mesmerized, my breath catching in my throat as she danced with raw, uninhibited passion.

She spun around the pole, her dress clinging to her body, accentuating every curve. With each movement, the dress inched higher, revealing her smooth, creamy thighs. I couldn't take my eyes off her, my desire for her growing with every sensuous twist and turn.

As the music reached its climax, Emily slid down the pole, her dress riding up, exposing her lacy black panties. She turned to face me, her eyes heavy with lust. With a sultry smile, she reached behind her back and slowly unzipped her dress, letting it fall to the floor, revealing her voluptuous body.

My mouth went dry as I took in the sight of her. Her large, soft breasts spilled from her bra, her nipples erect and begging for attention. Her stomach, once a source of insecurity, now looked like a beautiful, inviting canvas. Her hips swayed provocatively, drawing my gaze to her thick, round ass, covered only by the sheer fabric of her panties.

"You like what you see, papi?" she purred, her voice laced with desire.

I nodded, unable to form words as I stared at her, my cock throbbing painfully in my pants. Emily's eyes gleamed with satisfaction as she took a step towards me, her hands reaching for the buttons of my tux.

"Let's play a little game, Cameron," she whispered, her breath hot against my ear. "For every piece of clothing I remove, you have to throw some of our winnings at me."

I grinned, my heart racing with excitement. "I think I can handle that, beautiful."

Emily untied her bra, letting it fall to the floor, revealing her heavy breasts. I gasped, my eyes fixated on her nipples, already hard and begging for my touch. I reached into my pocket and pulled out a handful of chips, tossing them at her. The chips rained down on her body, some landing on her breasts, others on her stomach, and a few even finding their way into her panties.

She giggled, her hands reaching down to retrieve the chips, her fingers brushing against her sensitive skin. "Oh, papi, you're so naughty! Keep going."

I obliged, eagerly unbuttoning my shirt, revealing my bare chest. I threw more chips, aiming for her breasts, watching as they bounced off her nipples, sending shivers down her body. Emily's hands roamed over her body, caressing her breasts, pinching her nipples, and moaning softly.

"Now it's my turn," she whispered, her hands moving to my belt. With nimble fingers, she undid the buckle, sliding my belt free and letting it fall to the floor. She unzipped my pants, her hands sliding inside, grasping my hard cock through my boxers.

"Oh, Cameron, you're so big and hard," she murmured, her fingers stroking my length. "I want you so badly."

I groaned, my body on fire as her touch sent waves of pleasure through me. I reached for my wallet, pulling out a stack of bills, and threw them at her, watching as they fluttered down, covering her body.

Emily giggled, her eyes sparkling with mischief. "You're so generous, papi. Now, let's see what else you have for me."

She slid my pants and boxers down, freeing my throbbing cock. I stood before her, completely naked, my body on display. Emily's eyes widened as she took in the sight of my erection, her mouth watering.

"Mmm, you're so delicious, Cameron," she whispered, her hands reaching for my cock. She stroked me slowly, her touch firm and confident. "I want to taste you, papi. I want to feel you in my mouth."

I shuddered, my knees weak as she dropped to her knees before me. Her hands continued to stroke my shaft, her thumb swirling over the sensitive head, gathering the pre-cum that had begun to leak from my tip.

"Please, Emily," I begged, my voice hoarse with desire. "Suck me, baby. Take me into your mouth."

She smiled up at me, her eyes filled with lust. "Oh, I will, papi. I'll suck you so good."

With that, she leaned forward, her full lips parting to take me into her warm, wet mouth. Her tongue swirled around the head of my cock, teasing and tantalizing me. She took me deep, her throat constricting around my shaft, her hands caressing my balls, driving me wild with pleasure.

I moaned, my hands tangling in her hair, holding her in place as she sucked and licked me with abandon. Her mouth was hot and tight, and the sensation of her lips and tongue working my cock was almost too much to bear.

"Oh, fuck, Emily," I groaned, my hips thrusting forward, seeking more of her mouth. "You're gonna make me cum, baby. I'm so close."

Emily pulled back, her lips glistening with my precum. "Not yet, papi. I want to feel you cum in my pussy. I want you to fuck me on this pile of money we won."

I nodded, my heart racing as I picked her up in my arms, carrying her to the bed of money we had created. I laid her down gently, her body surrounded by the crisp bills, her eyes shining with desire.

"I want to taste you, too, Emily," I whispered, my fingers trailing down her body, caressing her soft skin. "Let me eat your pussy, baby."

She spread her legs wide, her wetness glistening in the dim light. I knelt between her thighs, my face inches from her core. I inhaled her scent, a heady mix of desire and arousal, and then I lowered my head, my tongue finding her clit.

I licked and sucked her sensitive bud, my fingers delving into her wetness, finding her sweet spot. Emily moaned, her hands gripping the sheets, her hips rising to meet my mouth. I devoured her, my tongue flicking and probing, driving her wild with pleasure.

"Oh, Cameron, yes! Right there!" she cried out, her body arching off the bed. "Don't stop, papi. Make me cum."

I obliged, my tongue working her clit relentlessly, my fingers thrusting in and out of her wet heat. Emily's moans filled the room, her body trembling as she rode the waves of pleasure I was giving her.

"I'm cumming, Cameron!" she screamed, her body convulsing as her orgasm hit her. I felt her juices flow over my fingers, her pussy clenching and releasing around them.

I smiled, my cock throbbing with need as I rose to my knees, positioning myself between her legs. Grabbing a condom from my pants, I ripped the foil package with my teeth and then rolled the latex down my hard shaft. I guided my hard dick to her entrance, teasing her with the tip, before thrusting forward, filling her in one smooth motion.

Emily gasped, her eyes rolling back as I filled her completely. I paused, letting her adjust to my size, before beginning a slow, steady rhythm, my hips pumping in and out of her tight heat.

"Oh, God, Cameron, you feel so good," she moaned, her hands gripping my ass, pulling me deeper into her. "Fuck me, papi. Make me cum again."

I obliged, my hands gripping her thick thighs, spreading her wide as I pounded into her, my balls slapping against her ass with each thrust.

Emily's moans turned to screams as I hit her sweet spot over and over, driving her to the brink of ecstasy.

"Yes, yes, yes!" she chanted, her body bucking against mine, her nails digging into my skin. "I'm cumming again, Cameron! Oh, fuck, I can't hold back!"

Her pussy clenched around my cock, milking me as her orgasm ripped through her. I felt her juices flow, coating my shaft, her body trembling beneath me. I held her tight, my own orgasm building to an unbearable peak.

"Emily, I'm cumming!" I groaned, my hips thrusting wildly as I emptied my load deep inside her. I felt her pussy contract around me, milking every drop of my cum, our bodies moving in perfect sync.

We lay there, breathless and spent, our bodies covered in sweat and the money we had won. Emily turned to me, her eyes filled with love and desire.

"I love you, Cameron," she whispered, her fingers tracing my face. "I never want this night to end."

I smiled, my heart overflowing with love for this incredible woman. "I love you too, Emily. And I promise, this is just the beginning of our adventure."

As we lay there, entangled in each other's arms, I knew that my life had changed forever. I had found love and passion with Emily, and I couldn't wait to see what the future held for us. The night had been magical, and I knew that with Emily by my side, every day would be an adventure, filled with love, laughter, and unforgettable memories.

Chapter 15

I couldn't believe how quickly things were progressing with Emily. After our incredible trip to Las Vegas, where we'd shared so many memorable moments, I was eager to introduce her to my world, to show her a different side of me. Little did I know that this decision would lead to a whirlwind of emotions and a house party that would change everything.

After flying back from Las Vegas, Emily suggested that we celebrate our new relationship with her family. I felt a surge of excitement and nervousness. I wanted to make a good impression on Emily's family, but more importantly, I wanted to show her that I could be more than just her friend. I wanted to be the man she deserved.

"So, Cam, you ready for this?" Emily asked, her dark eyes sparkling with mischief as she glanced at me from the passenger seat. Her curvy figure was accentuated by a vibrant floral dress, and her brunette hair danced in the wind as she rolled down the window, letting the warm breeze fill the car.

"As ready as I'll ever be," I replied, my voice cracking slightly. I adjusted my glasses, a nervous habit I couldn't seem to shake. "I liked meeting your family before, but I can't help feeling a bit anxious. I'm not your friend this time. I'm your boyfriend."

Emily reached over and squeezed my hand, her touch sending a jolt of electricity through my body. "They're going to love you, Cam. They're a bit crazy, but they're my crazy, and I adore them."

I smiled, feeling a surge of confidence from her words. Emily had this effect on me, making me believe in myself and my abilities. I was determined to make a good impression, not just for her, but for myself as well.

As we pulled up to her family's modest home in Virginia Beach, I could already hear the lively chatter and laughter coming from within. The scent of delicious Mexican food wafted through the open windows, and my stomach growled in anticipation. I had always loved the vibrant atmosphere of her culture, and I was eager to immerse myself in it.

Emily's family welcomed us with open arms, their warmth and hospitality instantly putting me at ease. Her parents, Mr. and Mrs. Lopez, greeted us with big smiles and hearty hugs. Her siblings, two older brothers and a younger sister, teased her playfully, making me feel like one of the gang immediately.

"Emily has told us so much about you, Cameron," Mrs. Lopez said, her kind eyes studying me. "We're so happy to finally meet the man who has brought a smile to our daughter's face."

I felt my cheeks heat up at her words, and I mumbled a humble thank you. Emily's brothers, Juan and Miguel, clapped me on the back, inviting me to join them for a game of soccer in the backyard. I was surprised by how quickly I felt at home with these strangers, who were now my extended family.

The afternoon was filled with laughter, delicious food, and lively conversations. I helped Emily's sister, Maria, prepare some traditional Mexican dishes, learning the secrets of her family's famous salsa recipe. Emily and I shared stories of our trip, and her family listened with rapt attention, asking questions and offering their own anecdotes.

As the sun began to set, the party showed no signs of slowing down. Emily's parents insisted that we stay for dinner, and soon the backyard was filled with the sounds of music and laughter. I found myself dancing with Emily, her body moving effortlessly to the rhythm, while I tried my best to keep up.

"You know, Cam, I never thought I'd see you dancing like this," Emily teased, her eyes sparkling with amusement. "You're usually so shy and reserved."

I laughed, feeling a bit self-conscious but also incredibly happy. "You bring out the best in me, Emily. I feel like I can do anything when I'm with you."

She leaned in and kissed me softly, her lips tasting like the margaritas we'd been sipping all evening. "I feel the same way, Cam. You make me feel special, and I want to show you how much I care."

My heart raced as I pulled her closer, the music and the moment aligning perfectly. I knew then that I was falling hard for Emily, and the thought of losing her to someone else was unbearable.

The party continued late into the night, and as the guests began to depart, Emily's parents suggested we all head to my place for an after-party. I was thrilled at the idea of showing them my home, but also nervous about how they would react to my wealth. I had always tried to keep a low profile, not wanting to draw attention to my financial status.

"Are you sure, Mr. and Mrs. Lopez? My place might be a bit different from what you're used to," I said, trying to sound casual.

Emily's father laughed, his eyes twinkling with mischief. "We'd love to see your home, Cameron. And don't worry, we won't judge you by your wealth. We're interested in getting to know you, not your bank account."

I breathed a sigh of relief, grateful for their understanding. As we all piled into our cars and made our way to my oceanfront home, I couldn't help but feel a sense of anticipation. I wanted to show them the best time, to make this night unforgettable.

As we arrived at my house, the modern architecture and sleek design stood in stark contrast to the cozy, traditional homes of Emily's neighborhood. I could see the awe on their faces as they took in the floor-to-ceiling windows and the breathtaking ocean views.

"Wow, Cam, this place is incredible!" Emily exclaimed, her eyes wide as she stepped inside. "I had no idea you lived in such a beautiful home."

I felt a bit embarrassed by the attention, but also proud to share this part of my life with her and her family. "It's not just a house, it's a sanctuary. I designed it to be a place where I can escape and relax."

Emily's parents and siblings explored the house, their voices filled with wonder as they discovered each unique feature. From the theater room with its popcorn maker and candy bar to the library filled with comic books and cozy reading nooks, they were like kids in a candy store.

"This is amazing, Cameron!" Maria exclaimed, her eyes lighting up as she ran her fingers along the spines of the comic books. "I had no idea you were such a fan."

I smiled, feeling a sense of connection with her. "It's one of my passions. I love escaping into these worlds, and I'm glad you appreciate it too."

As the night wore on, we gathered in the spacious kitchen, where I prepared a late-night feast. I cooked up a storm, making some of my favorite dishes, and Emily's family raved about my culinary skills. We laughed, told stories, and shared more about our lives, forming a bond that felt unbreakable.

"You know, Cameron, we're so glad Emily found you," Mr. Lopez said, raising his glass in a toast. "You've brought so much joy into our lives, and we can see how happy she is with you."

I felt my face flush with pleasure, and I looked at Emily, who was beaming with pride. "Thank you, Mr. Lopez. I feel the same way about your family. I'm honored to be a part of it."

As the sun began to rise over the ocean, casting a golden glow across the horizon, I found myself sitting on the plush outdoor sofa with Emily by my side. The party had finally wound down, and it was just the two of us, enjoying the peaceful morning.

"I can't believe how much has happened in the last few days," I said, my voice soft and filled with emotion. "I feel like I've found something special with you, Emily. Something I never thought I'd have."

Emily took my hand, her touch sending a wave of comfort through me. "I feel the same way, Cam. Being with you feels right. I've never met anyone like you, and I don't want to let you go."

I leaned in and kissed her, pouring all my love and desire into that moment. I knew then that I was falling deeply in love with Emily, and I couldn't wait to see what the future held for us.

As we sat there, watching the sunrise over the ocean, I realized that this was just the beginning of our journey together. The house party had brought us closer, and I was excited to see where our love would take us next. Little did I know, the best was yet to come.

Chapter 16

I woke up feeling refreshed, my eyes immediately drawn to the beautiful sight beside me. There she was, Emily Lopez, the woman who had turned my world upside down in the most delightful way. Her naked body lay sprawled across the bed, her curvy figure accentuated by the morning light streaming through the floor-to-ceiling windows of my beach house. I couldn't help but admire her—her soft, light tanned skin, her large, natural breasts, and her plump, round ass. It was a sight I never wanted to forget.

As I lay there, taking in her beauty, an overwhelming sense of longing washed over me. I wanted this every day. I wanted to wake up next to Emily, to start my mornings with her radiant smile and her warm embrace. I knew it might sound crazy, especially since we had only been dating for a couple of weeks, but I couldn't shake the feeling.

"Emily," I whispered, reaching out to touch her shoulder. "Wake up, beautiful."

She stirred, blinking her big brown eyes sleepily as she turned to face me. "Good morning, Cameron," she said, her voice husky with sleep. "Did you sleep well?"

"Better than I have in a long time," I replied, my heart already pounding with desire. "Emily, I need to tell you something."

She propped herself up on her elbow, her dark hair falling across her face, and gave me a curious look. "What is it, cariño?"

Gathering my courage, I took a deep breath. "I want you to move in with me. I know it's early in our relationship, but I can't imagine my life without you. I want to wake up to your gorgeous face every morning."

Emily's eyes widened, and for a moment, I thought I saw a spark of excitement in them. But then, her expression turned uncertain. "Cameron, we've only been dating for a short time. I mean, it's been amazing, but moving in together is a big step."

I felt my heart sink a little. I knew she had a point, but I couldn't help feeling disappointed. "I understand," I said, sitting up and running my hands through my messy afro. "I just thought... well, I thought you might feel the same way."

She reached out and placed her hand on my cheek, her touch soothing my disappointment. "I'm not saying never, Cameron. It's just... I need a little more time. I want to be sure this is the right decision for both of us."

I nodded, trying to hide my dejection. "Of course, I respect that. I just... I really like you, Emily. More than I've ever liked anyone."

A soft smile played on her lips. "I like you too, Cameron. A lot. And I want to take things slow, but in the right direction. Let's not rush into anything, okay?"

I sighed, knowing she was right. "Okay, I can be patient. I just hope you know how much I care about you."

Emily leaned in and kissed me gently, her lips soft and warm against mine. "I know, and I care about you too. Now, why don't you go take a shower, and I'll make us some breakfast? We can talk more later."

Her suggestion sounded like a good plan, so I reluctantly got out of bed, trying to hide my disappointment. I headed to the master bathroom, feeling the cool marble under my bare feet. The shower was exactly what I needed to clear my mind and ease the tension in my body.

As I stepped under the hot water, I let my thoughts wander. Emily and I had an incredible connection, and I knew I wanted her in my life permanently. I just had to be patient and let her come to the decision on her own.

After a refreshing shower, I wrapped a towel around my waist and walked back into the bedroom. I was surprised to find Emily already up and dressed, or rather, undressed. She stood in the kitchen, wearing nothing but a tiny apron that barely covered her voluptuous curves.

Her back was turned to me, and she was busy cooking something on the stove.

"Emily?" I called out, my voice cracking slightly at the sight before me. "What are you doing?"

She turned around, a mischievous smile on her face. "I thought about what you said, Cameron, and I changed my mind. I want to move in. I'm making breakfast to make up for our little fight earlier."

I couldn't believe my ears. "You... you're moving in? Just like that?"

She giggled, her brown eyes sparkling with amusement. "Well, not just like that, papi. But yes, I've decided I want to take a chance on us. And I thought, what better way to start than with a delicious breakfast?"

I felt a surge of happiness and relief wash over me. "That's amazing, Emily! I can't tell you how happy this makes me."

She winked at me. "Well, I can think of one way to show me how happy you are."

I raised an eyebrow, my mind already racing with possibilities. "Oh yeah? And what's that?"

Emily's smile turned seductive as she untied her apron and let it drop to the floor, revealing her naked body once again. "I want you, Cameron. Right here, right now."

My mouth went dry as I took in the sight of her standing there, completely exposed and utterly desirable. I didn't need any further invitation. I strode across the kitchen, my towel falling to the floor, and pulled her close to me.

"I want you too, Emily," I whispered, my voice hoarse with desire. "More than you know."

Our lips met in a feverish kiss, tongues entwining as we explored each other's mouths. I ran my hands over her soft skin, cupping her breasts and feeling her nipples harden under my touch. She moaned into my mouth, her hands gripping my shoulders, pulling me closer.

Breaking away for a moment, I lifted her up and sat her on the kitchen counter, her legs wrapping around my waist. I kissed her neck, trailing kisses down to her breasts, taking one nipple into my mouth and sucking gently. Emily arched her back, her hands threading through my afro, pulling me closer to her.

"Oh, Cameron," she breathed, her voice a mixture of pleasure and surprise. "You're making me so wet."

I smiled against her breast, my hands exploring her soft curves. "That's the idea, gorgeous. I want to make you feel good."

I kissed my way down her stomach, pausing to appreciate the sight of her plump belly and the soft, dark curls between her thighs. I inhaled her scent, a mixture of arousal and Emily's natural musk, and it drove me wild.

"Please, Cameron," she whispered, her fingers tangling in my hair. "I need you inside me."

"Did you want me to get a condom?"

"Not this time."

"Are you sure?"

"Yes, I want to feel you. All of you."

"As you wish..."

I looked up at her, my eyes locking with hers, and saw the raw desire burning in her gaze. I wanted to give her what she craved, to make her feel the same pleasure I was experiencing.

Positioning myself between her legs, I guided my throbbing cock to her entrance, feeling her wetness as I teased her with the tip. Emily's breath caught, and she bit her lip, her eyes never leaving mine.

"Fuck me, Cameron," she pleaded, her voice thick with need. "Please, I can't wait anymore."

With one smooth thrust, I slid into her, filling her completely. She gasped, her back arching off the counter, her breasts swaying with the motion. I paused, letting her adjust to my size, before beginning a slow, rhythmic pace.

"You feel so good, Emily," I groaned, my hands gripping her thighs. "So tight and warm."

She moaned in response, her hands grasping the edge of the counter, her nails digging into the wood. "Yes, papi, just like that. Harder, please."

I obliged, picking up the pace and thrusting into her with more force, my balls slapping against her ass with each stroke. Emily's moans filled the kitchen, a mixture of Spanish and English, as she urged me on.

"Yes, yes, like that! Oh, fuck, Cameron, you're making me come!"

Her words spurred me on, and I drove into her with abandon, my own orgasm building to an intense peak. I felt her walls clench around me, her pussy gripping my cock as she came, her juices flowing around me.

"Emily!" I cried out, my voice hoarse as I emptied myself into her, my body shaking with the force of my release.

We stayed locked together, our hearts racing and our bodies slick with sweat. I kissed her, tasting myself on her lips, and she smiled up at me, her eyes sparkling with satisfaction.

"That was incredible," she whispered, running her fingers through my hair. "I think I've made the right decision, moving in with you."

I chuckled, my heart filled with joy. "I think so too, mi amor. And this is just the beginning."

Emily giggled, her eyes sparkling with mischief. "I can't wait to see what else you have in store for me, Cameron Briggs. I have a feeling this is going to be one hell of a ride."

Little did I know, she was absolutely right. Our relationship was about to take some unexpected turns, and I was ready to embrace every thrilling moment with this incredible woman by my side.

Chapter 17

I couldn't take my eyes off Emily as we sat on the cozy couch in my beach house, the glow of the TV illuminating our faces. There was something about how sexy she looked in her spaghetti tank top and short shorts. We had just finished watching our favorite fantasy show, and the tension between us was palpable. Emily's eyes sparkled with mischief, and I knew something was up when she started giggling.

"I can't believe how much that show turns me on," she said, her voice laced with a playful tone. "That barbaric king and his conquests... it's so hot!"

I felt my cheeks warm at her words. "Yeah, it's quite the show. I mean, the way they portray those medieval times..." I trailed off, not wanting to admit that I found the scenes just as arousing.

"Oh, come on, Cameron," she teased, reading my thoughts. "You think it's sexy too. Admit it."

I couldn't deny it any longer. "Alright, fine. It's pretty damn hot. But I didn't expect you to be into it. You seem to be fully invested into the geek culture. Comic con now my favorite fantasy tv show..."

Emily laughed, her brown eyes sparkling with amusement. "Of course, papi. I love you. At first I thought it was a little weird for a grown man to be into comic books, but now I like it. I like the action and the visuals. I also like how much you're into it. I think it's sexy."

I felt my heart flutter at her words. "Well, you are pretty damn sexy, Emily Lopez. There, I said it."

She leaned closer, her scent intoxicating. "And what if I told you I want to act out one of those scenes? You know, role-play a little?"

My breath caught in my throat. I had never done anything like that before, but the thought of Emily in a medieval fantasy role-play was enough to make my pulse race. "What did you have in mind, my lady?" I asked, playing along.

"Watching that barbaric king take his virgin bride was so intense. I want to be that bride, and you, my dear king, will have your way with me." She bit her lower lip, her eyes daring me to accept the challenge.

I stood up, feeling a surge of confidence. "Then let the role-play begin, my queen. I shall be the barbaric king you desire."

Emily's eyes widened with excitement as I took her hand and led her towards the master bedroom. The room was dimly lit, with the soft glow of the setting sun filtering through the floor-to-ceiling windows, casting a warm ambiance. The white marble countertops and heated floors added to the luxurious atmosphere.

"Kneel before your king, my lady," I commanded, my voice taking on a deeper, more authoritative tone. Emily's playful expression turned to one of feigned obedience as she sank to her knees in front of me.

"Your wish is my command, my lord," she said, her voice laced with mock submission.

I stepped closer, my eyes fixed on her beautiful face. "You are my queen, and I shall treat you as such. But first, I must prepare you for my pleasure."

With that, I began to undress her, slowly and deliberately. I pulled away her tank top, revealing her plump, creamy breasts. Her brown nipples hardened in the cool air, and I couldn't resist leaning down to take one into my mouth. Emily gasped as I sucked and teased her sensitive peak, her hands gripping my shoulders.

"Oh, my king," she moaned, her voice breathy. "Your touch is divine."

I moved to the other breast, lavishing it with the same attention, while my hands explored her curvy body. Her skin was soft and warm, and I couldn't get enough of her. I trailed kisses down her neck, nipping gently at her sensitive skin, making her squirm with pleasure.

"Please, my lord," she whispered, her voice hoarse. "Take me now."

I stood up, my body throbbing with desire. "Not yet, my queen. You must be prepared for my royal staff."

Emily's eyes widened as I reached for the bedside drawer and pulled out a small velvet box. Inside was a delicate lace blindfold and a pair of soft silk restraints.

"What are those for, my king?" she asked, her voice laced with curiosity and a hint of nervousness.

"To heighten your senses, my love," I replied, my voice low and husky. "You will see nothing, but feel everything."

I gently tied the blindfold around her eyes, plunging her into darkness. Her breathing quickened, and I could sense her anticipation. I secured her wrists with the silk restraints, attaching them to the bedposts, ensuring she was comfortable.

"Trust me, my queen," I whispered, my lips brushing against her ear. "I will take care of you."

I began to explore her body with my hands, tracing her curves, caressing her soft skin. I kissed her neck, her shoulders, and made my way down her body, leaving a trail of kisses and gentle bites. I teased her nipples with my tongue, sucking and nibbling, making her arch her back and moan in pleasure.

"Oh, Cameron," she whispered, her voice strained. "This is incredible."

I moved lower, kissing her stomach, her hips, and finally reaching the apex of her thighs. I could feel her heat and wetness through the thin fabric of her panties. I hooked my fingers under the elastic and slowly slid them down her legs, revealing her glistening pussy.

"You're so beautiful, my queen," I murmured, my voice thick with desire. "So wet and ready for me."

I blew gently on her sensitive flesh, making her shiver and moan. I kissed her inner thighs, teasing her, before finally taking her clit into my mouth. I sucked and licked, driving her wild with pleasure. Emily writhed against the restraints, her hips bucking as I brought her closer and closer to the edge.

"Oh, my king, I'm going to..." she gasped, her body tensing.

I increased the pace, my tongue flicking against her sweet spot, and Emily cried out, her orgasm crashing over her. Her juices flowed freely, and I lapped them up, savoring her taste.

"That was incredible," she panted, her chest heaving. "I've never felt anything like that."

I released her from the restraints and blindfold, gazing into her lust-filled eyes. "You are incredible, my love. But the night is not over yet."

I stood up, shedding my clothes, revealing my hard, throbbing cock. Emily's eyes widened at the sight, and she licked her lips hungrily.

"My lord, you are a sight to behold," she purred, reaching out to stroke my length.

I groaned as her soft hand wrapped around me, her touch sending sparks of pleasure through my body. "You have no idea how long I've wanted to feel you inside me," she whispered.

I climbed onto the bed, positioning myself between her thighs. "Then let me make your fantasy come true, my queen."

I guided my cock to her entrance, feeling her wetness envelop me. I thrust forward, filling her in one smooth motion. Emily gasped, her eyes rolling back as she adjusted to my size.

"You're so big," she whispered, her hands gripping my shoulders. "But it feels so good."

I began to move, slowly at first, savoring the sensation of being inside her. I withdrew almost completely before thrusting deep, hitting her sweet spot. Emily moaned, her nails digging into my back.

"Harder, my king," she begged. "Take me like the barbaric king you are."

I obliged, picking up the pace, my hips slamming into hers. The sound of our bodies slapping together filled the room, mingling with our moans and gasps. I leaned down, capturing her lips in a passionate kiss, our tongues dancing wildly.

"You feel so good, Emily," I groaned between kisses. "I can't get enough of you."

She wrapped her legs around my waist, urging me deeper. "I want to feel you come inside me, Cameron. I want to be yours."

Her words sent me over the edge. I thrust harder, faster, my balls slapping against her ass. I could feel my orgasm building, an intense pressure coiling in my groin.

"I'm close, baby," I grunted, my breath coming in short gasps. "So close."

Emily's pussy clenched around me, milking my cock as she climaxed again, her walls rippling with pleasure. I couldn't hold back any longer, and with a final, powerful thrust, I emptied myself into her, filling her with my hot cum.

We lay there, entangled in each other's arms, our hearts racing and our bodies glistening with sweat. I kissed her forehead, feeling a sense of contentment wash over me.

"That was... incredible," I managed to say, my voice hoarse. "I've never experienced anything like that."

Emily smiled, her eyes sparkling. "I'm so glad we did this, Cameron. It was amazing."

I propped myself up on my elbow, gazing down at her beautiful face. "You know, Scotland has some of the most incredible castles. I've always wanted to visit them."

Emily's eyes widened with excitement. "Scotland? You mean like the ones in the show? That would be amazing!"

I smiled, feeling a surge of joy. "Then let's do it. We can plan a trip, just you and me. It'll be our own little adventure."

She threw her arms around my neck, pulling me into a tight embrace. "I'd love that, Cameron. I've always wanted to go to Europe, and I've always wanted to see those castles. It'll be our romantic getaway."

I held her close, my heart swelling with love. "I love you, Emily Lopez. And I can't wait to explore the world with you."

She kissed me softly, her lips tasting of passion and desire. "I love you too, Cameron Briggs. And I can't wait to see what other adventures we'll have together."

As we lay there, snuggled in each other's arms, I knew that our love story was just beginning. The thought of exploring Scotland's castles with Emily by my side filled me with excitement and anticipation. Our journey together was just getting started, and I couldn't wait to see what the future held for us.

Chapter 18

I couldn't believe what was happening. There we were, Emily and I, packing our bags for our much-anticipated trip to Scotland, when she suddenly turned pale and rushed to the bathroom, feeling nauseous. I was concerned, but little did I know that this would be the start of an even more life-changing journey for us.

As I knocked on the bathroom door, a mix of worry and confusion swirling in my mind, Emily's voice, slightly trembling, responded. "Cam, I think I might be pregnant." My heart skipped a beat. I had never considered the possibility, but then again, our relationship had been moving at a whirlwind pace. We had only known each other for a few months, but it felt like I had known her my entire life.

"Are you sure, Em? Should we get a test?" I asked, my voice filled with concern. I wanted to be there for her, to support her no matter what.

"Yes, please. I need to know for sure," she replied, her voice cracking. I rushed out to the nearest pharmacy, my mind racing with thoughts. Emily and I had been careful, but accidents happen, and I knew that she had a past experience with an unplanned pregnancy. I wanted to be there for her, to show her that I was different from the guy who had hurt her before.

I returned with the pregnancy test, my hands shaking slightly as I handed it to her. We waited anxiously, sitting side by side on the couch in my oceanfront home. The silence between us was filled with unspoken questions and emotions. I held her hand, giving it a gentle squeeze, hoping to provide some comfort.

After what felt like an eternity, Emily emerged from the bathroom, her beautiful brown eyes glistening with unshed tears. "It's positive, Cam. I'm pregnant." My heart sank, not because I didn't want a child, but because I knew this would be a huge decision for Emily. She had dreams and aspirations, and I wanted to make sure she felt supported and loved.

"Oh, Em... I..." I struggled to find the right words, not wanting to pressure her. "I want you to know that I'm here for you, no matter what you decide. We can figure this out together."

Emily smiled through her tears, taking my hand in hers. "I know, Cam. I'm just... I never thought this would happen so soon. I want to keep the baby, but I also want to do right by you. I don't want to rush into anything."

I leaned in and kissed her softly, my heart overflowing with love and admiration for this incredible woman. "Em, I want you to know that I love you. And I want to spend the rest of my life with you. I was planning to ask you on our trip, but I think now is the perfect time."

Her eyes widened, and a mix of emotions played across her face. "Cam, are you sure? I mean, we've only been together for a few months. What about your trip? And what if I'm not the right person for you?"

I chuckled, taking her hands in mine. "Emily Lopez, you are the most amazing woman I've ever met. You've brought color and joy into my life, and I can't imagine spending a day without you. As for the trip, we can always go another time. But right now, I want to make you my wife."

Emily's eyes sparkled with happiness, and she threw her arms around me, burying her face in my neck. "Yes, Cam. Yes, I will marry you. I love you so much, and I can't wait to start a family with you."

I picked her up in my arms, carrying her to the master bedroom, our laughter filling the air. As I laid her down on the soft bed, I couldn't help but admire her beauty. Her curvy figure, with her large, soft breasts and round ass, was a sight to behold. I wanted to worship her body, to show her how much I desired her.

"Cam, you're still fully dressed," she giggled, reaching for my belt. I quickly undressed, my glasses falling to the side as I revealed my lean, muscular body. I had been working out regularly, wanting to be in the best shape for Emily.

"You're so sexy, papi," she purred, her hands running down my chest, making me shiver with anticipation. I kissed her passionately, our tongues dancing in a familiar rhythm. My hands cupped her breasts, squeezing them gently, feeling the weight of them in my palms. Emily moaned into my mouth, her hands tugging at my hair.

I broke the kiss, trailing my lips down her neck, leaving a trail of kisses and soft bites. "You taste so good, mi amor," I whispered, my breath hot against her skin. I sucked on her sensitive skin, making her squirm beneath me.

"Oh, Cam... right there," she moaned, her hands gripping the sheets. I continued my descent, kissing and licking my way down her body, until I reached her plump breasts. I took one nipple into my mouth, suckling it gently, then switching to the other, teasing them with my tongue.

Emily's back arched off the bed, her hands tangled in my hair, guiding me. "Yes, papi, suck them. They're all yours." I smiled against her skin, loving the way she surrendered to me. I lavished attention on her breasts, paying homage to every inch of her soft, supple flesh.

My hands roamed lower, caressing her thighs, slowly inching towards her core. I could feel her heat through her panties, and I wanted to taste her, to drive her wild with pleasure. With a swift motion, I ripped her panties off, exposing her glistening pussy.

"Oh, papi, you're so naughty," she giggled, her cheeks flushed with desire. I gazed at her beautiful pussy, the lips already swollen and parted, revealing her glistening inner folds. I inhaled her scent, a mix of musk and arousal, driving me wild.

I dove in, my tongue seeking out her clit, flicking it gently at first, then increasing the pace as she squirmed and moaned beneath me. "Yes, Cam, right there. Oh, God, that feels so good." Her words spurred me on, and I devoured her pussy, licking and sucking, driving her closer to the edge.

I inserted a finger into her wetness, curling it upwards, searching for that sweet spot that would send her over the edge. "Oh, fuck, Cam! I'm gonna cum!" she cried out, her body tensing as her orgasm built. I sucked her clit into my mouth, my finger working in sync, and Emily came undone, her juices flooding my mouth and chin.

I lapped up her essence, savoring the taste of her pleasure. I kissed my way back up her body, stopping to nibble on her earlobe. "You taste so sweet, mi amor. I want to feel you around me."

Emily's eyes smoldered with desire, her hands reaching for my throbbing cock. "I want you inside me, papi. Make me yours." I positioned myself between her thighs, my cock brushing against her wetness, teasing her entrance.

"Please, Cam, I need you," she pleaded, her hips rising to meet mine. I thrust forward, filling her in one smooth motion, our bodies becoming one. Emily gasped, her eyes rolling back as she adjusted to my size.

"You feel so good, Em. So fucking tight," I groaned, my hips moving in a slow, rhythmic pace. I wanted to savor this moment, to make our first time as husband and wife unforgettable.

Emily wrapped her legs around my waist, pulling me deeper into her. "Harder, papi. Fuck me harder," she demanded, her nails digging into my back. I obliged, my thrusts becoming more urgent, my cock pounding into her wet heat.

"Oh, yes! Right there, Cam. I'm close," she panted, her pussy clenching around my shaft. I felt her walls pulsating, signaling her impending release. I quickened my pace, my balls slapping against her ass, driving her wild.

"I'm cumming, Cam! Oh, God, I'm cumming!" Emily cried out, her body trembling as her orgasm washed over her. I held her tightly, my cock buried deep within her, as I felt my own release building.

"Em, I'm gonna cum too," I grunted, my hips moving frantically. I pulled out, my cock glistening with her juices, and stroked myself as I watched her beautiful face contort in pleasure.

"Cum for me, papi. Let me see it," she begged, her fingers playing with her clit, prolonging her orgasm. I obliged, my hand moving furiously, and with a guttural groan, I shot my hot cum all over her breasts and stomach, painting her with my desire.

We lay there, entangled in each other's arms, our hearts racing and our bodies glistening with sweat and cum. "I love you, Emily Lopez. And I can't wait to spend the rest of our lives together," I whispered, kissing her softly.

She smiled, her eyes sparkling with happiness. "I love you too, Cameron Briggs. And I can't wait to start our family. But first, let's clean up this mess we made, and then we can celebrate our engagement properly."

I chuckled, pulling her close for another kiss. "I think we've already started the celebration, mi amor. And I can't wait to see what the future holds for us."

Little did we know, our journey was about to take an even more unexpected turn, one that would test our love and commitment in ways we never imagined. But for now, we savored the sweetness of our newfound love, knowing that the best was yet to come.

Chapter 19

I stood at the altar, my heart pounding with anticipation as I waited for my bride. The sun shone brightly through the stained-glass windows of the quaint little church, casting a warm glow on the white rose petals scattered down the aisle. I adjusted my black tuxedo, straightening the sleeves, feeling a bit out of my element in this formal attire. But today wasn't about me; it was about Emily and our love story.

As the guests turned to look, the sound of a traditional Mexican wedding march filled the air, signaling the start of the ceremony. My eyes widened as I caught the first glimpse of Emily. She was a vision in white, her plus-sized figure accentuated by a stunning lace gown that hugged her curves in all the right places. Her brunette hair, styled in soft curls, fell gracefully onto her shoulders, and her light tanned skin glowed with happiness.

I couldn't help but smile as she gracefully made her way down the aisle, her eyes sparkling with joy. Emily's beauty took my breath away, and in that moment, I knew I was the luckiest man alive. She looked so different from the first time we met, when she was dressed casually in her waitress uniform at Los Amigos. Today, she was a radiant bride, and I couldn't wait to call her my wife.

As she approached, I noticed the nervousness in her eyes, a contrast to her usual outgoing demeanor. I gave her a reassuring smile, hoping to ease her nerves. Emily's walk down the aisle seemed to take an eternity, and I was eager to reach out and take her hand. Finally, she stood by my side, and I whispered, "You look absolutely breathtaking, Emily."

Her cheeks flushed, and she responded with a giggle, "Ay, papi, you're gonna make me blush. I feel like a princess today."

The ceremony began, and the pastor's words echoed through the church, reminding us of the significance of the vows we were about to exchange. I held Emily's hand tightly, feeling the warmth of her skin against mine. When the time came for our vows, I spoke from the heart, my voice steady despite the emotions swirling within me.

"Emily, from the moment I met you, you brought color and joy into my life. You taught me how to love and be loved. I promise to always be by your side, to support you, and to cherish every moment we have together. I will love you through the good times and the bad, and I can't wait to build a future filled with laughter, adventure, and endless love."

My words seemed to touch her deeply, and tears of happiness welled up in her eyes. She took a deep breath before responding, her voice shaking slightly.

"Cameron, my dear, sweet Cameron. You came into my life when I least expected it, and you showed me that fairytales can come true. You've loved me for who I am, and you've never tried to change me. I promise to be your partner in crime, to dance with you through life, and to always bring a smile to your face. I will love you fiercely, and I can't wait to explore the world with you by my side."

The pastor pronounced us husband and wife, and as we exchanged rings, I felt a surge of happiness and relief. We sealed our union with a passionate kiss, and the guests erupted in cheers and applause.

The reception that followed was a vibrant celebration of our love. The beachside venue was adorned with colorful flowers and twinkling fairy lights, creating a magical atmosphere. Emily and I shared our first dance as husband and wife, swaying to a romantic ballad. Her body pressed against mine, and I could feel her heart racing. We laughed and whispered sweet nothings in each other's ears, lost in our own little world.

Throughout the night, we mingled with our guests, many of whom had traveled from afar to celebrate with us. Emily's large family added a lively touch to the festivities, filling the air with laughter and music. They welcomed me with open arms, making me feel like I was one of their own. As we danced and celebrated, I couldn't help but notice the joy and love radiating from Emily's face. She was in her element, surrounded by the people she loved.

After cutting the three-tiered wedding cake, Emily and I snuck away for a moment of privacy. We found ourselves on the beach, the soft sand beneath our feet and the sound of the waves crashing against the shore. The moonlight illuminated Emily's face, making her look even more ethereal. I pulled her close, my hands resting on her waist, and whispered, "I love you, Mrs. Briggs."

She giggled, her eyes sparkling with mischief. "And I love you, Mr. Briggs. But you know, I think I prefer the sound of 'Emily Lopez' a little bit more. It has a nice ring to it, don't you think?"

I smiled, brushing a stray hair from her face. "I love the sound of your name, Emily Lopez. It's the name of the woman who stole my heart and changed my life forever."

As I leaned in for another kiss, Emily pulled back playfully, her eyes glinting with desire. "Oh, Mr. Briggs, you're such a romantic. But I think it's time we retire to our honeymoon suite. I have a feeling this night is going to get even better."

Hand in hand, we made our way back to the hotel, our laughter echoing through the night. The suite was adorned with rose petals and candles, creating an intimate ambiance. As we entered, Emily's eyes lit up with excitement. She ran her fingers through the petals on the bed, her smile widening.

"Oh, Cameron, it's perfect. I can't believe we're finally here, on our honeymoon."

I wrapped my arms around her from behind, my lips brushing her neck. "It's only the beginning, my love. We have a lifetime of adventures ahead of us."

As I turned her around, our lips met in a passionate kiss, igniting a flame between us. Emily's hands roamed over my body, her touch sending shivers down my spine. I unbuttoned her dress, revealing her voluptuous curves, and she helped me out of my tuxedo, our clothes falling to the floor in a hurried mess.

We tumbled onto the bed, our bodies entwined in a dance of desire. I explored every inch of her, my hands caressing her soft skin, her curves driving me wild. Emily's moans filled the room as I kissed my way down her body, paying homage to every part of her. Her scent, a mix of perfume and the ocean breeze intoxicated my senses.

"Papi, you're driving me crazy," she whispered, her breath hot against my ear. "Take me, make me yours."

I positioned myself between her thighs, gazing into her lust-filled eyes. "I want to make this moment last forever, Emily. I want to give you pleasure beyond your wildest dreams."

With that, I entered her slowly, savoring the sensation of becoming one with my wife. Emily arched her back, her hands gripping the sheets, as I began to move in a rhythmic motion. Our bodies moved in perfect harmony, each thrust eliciting moans of pleasure from her lips.

"Oh, Cameron, yes! Right there, papi, don't stop," she cried out, her voice hoarse with desire.

I quickened my pace, driven by the need to bring her to the brink of ecstasy. Emily's body tensed, and her nails dug into my back as she climaxed, her release flooding over me. I continued to move, determined to give her more, and soon, we were both lost in a whirlwind of pleasure, our cries of passion filling the room.

As our bodies calmed, I collapsed onto the bed beside her, my heart still racing. Emily turned to me, her eyes glistening with post-coital satisfaction.

"That was incredible, my love. I never imagined our first time could be so perfect," she said, tracing my lips with her finger.

I smiled, my heart overflowing with love. "It's only the beginning, Emily. We have a lifetime of pleasure and discovery ahead of us. I can't wait to explore every inch of your beautiful body and give you all the love and passion you deserve."

Emily giggled, her cheeks flushed with pleasure. "And I can't wait to explore yours, Mr. Briggs. I have a feeling this honeymoon to Scotland is going to be one wild ride."

"I can't wait."

Little did we know that our honeymoon to Scotland would be just the start of an adventure filled with love, passion, and unexpected twists. But for now, we were content to revel in the bliss of our newfound marriage, making memories that would last a lifetime.

***

The days that followed in Edinburgh, Scotland were blur of passion and exploration. We spent our mornings lazing in bed, making love under the warm sun streaming through the windows. Afternoons were spent on exploring the town and the castles in the surrounding area. We went to three different castle and also visited a nearby renaissance festival. In the evenings, we dined at romantic restaurants, savoring delicious meals and sharing stories of our pasts and dreams for the future.

One night, after a particularly romantic dinner, we found ourselves back in our suite, lost in each other's arms. Emily, ever the playful temptress, had a mischievous glint in her eye as she led me to the bed.

"I have a surprise for you, papi," she whispered, her voice laced with anticipation.

Intrigued, I allowed her to take the lead, my curiosity piqued. Emily blindfolded me gently, her hands guiding me to the bed. I could hear her moving around the room, the sound of her footsteps sending a thrill through my body.

"Trust me, Cameron," she said, her breath warm against my ear. "I want to give you something special."

I felt her hands on my chest, her touch sending shivers down my spine. She began to undress me slowly, her lips trailing kisses along my neck and shoulders. I was helpless to resist as she teased and tantalized me, my body responding to her every touch.

"You're so beautiful, Emily," I managed to whisper, my voice hoarse with desire.

"Not as beautiful as you, papi. You are my king and I aim to please you like one..." she replied, her hands skillfully removing my clothes.

Soon, I was naked, my body on fire with anticipation. Emily's hands roamed over my skin, her touch both gentle and firm. She kissed her way down my body, her tongue tracing patterns on my chest and stomach, driving me wild with desire.

"Oh, Emily, what are you doing to me?" I groaned, my hands reaching out to touch her.

"Shh, just relax and let me take care of you, you are my king and I am your queen..." she whispered, her breath hot against my skin.

I grinned remembering our foreplay of barbaric king and queen.

"As you wish my queen." I smirked, playing along.

I felt her lips wrap around my stiffness, her mouth warm and wet. She took me in deeply, her tongue swirling and teasing, sending waves of pleasure through my body. I arched my back, my hands gripping the sheets as I struggled to control my urges.

"My queen, you're incredible," I gasped, my voice laced with pleasure.

She continued her sensual assault, her hands and mouth working in perfect harmony. I was lost in a haze of sensation, my body trembling on the edge of release.

"That's it, papi, let it all out," she whispered, her voice a soft encouragement.

I climaxed with a guttural cry, my body convulsing as wave after wave of pleasure washed over me. Emily continued her ministrations, milking every last drop of pleasure from my body.

Finally, I collapsed back onto the bed, my heart pounding and my body sated. Emily removed the blindfold, her eyes sparkling with satisfaction.

"How was that, my love?" she asked, her voice filled with tenderness.

I pulled her close, my arms wrapping around her. "You're amazing, Emily. I've never experienced anything like that before."

She giggled, her cheeks flushed with pleasure. "I'm glad you enjoyed it, papi. I wanted to show you how much I love you and how much I want to pleasure you."

We spent the rest of the night entwined in each other's arms, our bodies exhausted but content. The following day, we decided to explore the vibrant of Edinburgh. We strolled along the bustling town, hand in hand, stopping to admire the street performers and sample the local cuisine.

As we walked, Emily's hand slipped into mine, her touch grounding me in the midst of the small Scottish town. We stopped to watch a street artist painting a colorful mural, and Emily's eyes lit up with excitement.

"Oh, Cameron, look at this! Isn't it beautiful?" she exclaimed, pointing to the vibrant artwork.

I smiled, admiring the intricate details of the painting. "It's incredible, Emily. I love how it captures the energy of the city."

We spent a few moments watching the artist at work, lost in the creative process. As we continued our walk, Emily's attention was suddenly drawn to a small boutique shop selling handmade jewelry.

"Oh, papi, can we go in? I want to get you something special," she said, her eyes sparkling with mischief.

Intrigued, I followed her into the shop, the bell above the door jingling as we entered. The store was filled with unique, handcrafted pieces, each one more beautiful than the last. Emily's eyes lit up as she browsed the displays, her fingers gently caressing the delicate necklaces and bracelets.

"I want to get you something that represents our love, something you can wear and think of me," she said, her voice filled with affection.

I smiled, touched by her thoughtfulness. "You don't have to get me anything, Emily. Just having you by my side is the greatest gift."

She shook her head, her determination unwavering. "No, I want to do this for you. I want to find the perfect piece that symbolizes our connection."

We spent the next hour exploring the shop, Emily carefully selecting a few items for me to try on. I stood patiently as she placed a leather bracelet on my wrist, her fingers brushing against my skin.

"This one is perfect, papi," she said, her eyes sparkling with delight. "It's strong and rugged, just like you, but with a touch of elegance."

I looked down at the bracelet, admiring the intricate design. "It's beautiful, Emily. I'll treasure it always."

She beamed with pride, her face glowing with happiness. "I'm so glad you like it. Now, whenever you wear it, you'll think of me and our love."

As we left the shop, hand in hand, I couldn't help but feel a sense of contentment. Emily's thoughtful gesture had touched my heart, and the bracelet on my wrist served as a tangible reminder of our love.

The days of our honeymoon flew by in a whirlwind of passion, laughter, and new experiences. As our time in Scotland came to an end, we packed our bags, our hearts filled with memories and our love for each other stronger than ever.

On our final night, we decided to indulge in a romantic dinner at a rooftop restaurant overlooking the hills. The sunset painted the sky in hues of orange and pink, creating a breathtaking backdrop for our last evening together.

As we sat at our table, Emily's eyes sparkled with emotion. "I can't believe our honeymoon is almost over, Cameron. It's been the most incredible time of my life."

I reached across the table, taking her hand in mine. "It's been perfect, Emily. But it's just the beginning. We have a lifetime of adventures ahead of us."

She smiled, her eyes glistening with unshed tears. "I know, papi. And I can't wait to experience it all with you by my side."

We savored our meal, sharing stories of our favorite moments from the past week. As the sun dipped below the horizon, casting a golden glow over the city, I felt a sense of peace and contentment wash over me.

"Emily, I have something for you," I said, reaching into my pocket and pulling out a small velvet box.

Her eyes widened with surprise, and she gasped softly. "Cameron, what is it?"

I opened the box, revealing a pair of diamond earrings, their brilliance sparkling in the fading light. "I wanted to give you something special, something to remind you of our love and this incredible journey we've shared."

Tears welled up in her eyes as she took the box from my hands. "Oh, Cameron, they're beautiful. I can't believe you did this."

I took the earrings from the box and gently placed them on her ears, my fingers brushing against her soft skin. "They're perfect for you, Emily. Just like you're perfect for me."

She turned her head, admiring the earrings in the mirror. "I love them, Cameron. I'll cherish them forever."

We embraced, our hearts filled with love and gratitude. After gazing at the city lights twinkling below, we retired to our cozy cabin, eager to explore each other's bodies. The air was crisp, and a fire crackled in the fireplace, setting the perfect ambiance for our passionate encounter.

Emily, my curvy goddess, wore a sexy silk robe that barely contained her ample assets. Her dark eyes sparkled with desire as she approached me, her full lips curving into a mischievous smile. I felt my dick stir in my jeans, already hardening at the thought of what was to come.

"Mmm, Papi," she purred, running her hands through my afro, "You look so handsome, and I can see you're ready for me." Her fingers trailed down my chest, making my breath catch in my throat. I wanted her so badly, and the anticipation was killing me.

I pulled her close, my hands sliding down her soft curves, cupping her plump ass through the silk. "I've been thinking about this all day, baby," I whispered, my voice hoarse with need. "I want to make this night unforgettable."

Emily giggled, a playful glint in her eyes. "Then let's not waste any time, mi amor." With a swift motion, she untied her robe, letting it fall to the floor, revealing her naked body. Her large, soft breasts swayed with the movement, and her dark nipples were already puckered with arousal.

I groaned, my dick throbbing against my zipper. I pushed her gently onto the bed, following her down, my lips seeking hers. Our tongues danced wildly, tasting each other, as I ground my erection against her warm thigh. She moaned into my mouth, her hands tugging at my shirt, eager to feel my skin.

Quickly, I stripped off my clothes, unable to contain my excitement any longer. My cock sprang free, standing erect and ready for her. Emily's eyes widened at the sight, and she licked her lips hungrily.

"Oh, Cameron, you're so big," she breathed, reaching out to stroke my length. "I want you inside me. Now."

I positioned myself between her thighs, my dick brushing against her wet pussy lips. She was already dripping, her juices coating my shaft as I teased her entrance. "You feel so fucking good, Emily," I grunted, thrusting my hips forward, but not entering her yet.

"Please, Papi, fuck me already!" she begged, her accent thick with lust. "I need your cock in my pussy."

I plunged into her, filling her tight hole in one swift motion. Emily cried out, her nails digging into my back as she wrapped her legs around my waist, pulling me deeper. The sensation was incredible; her pussy clenched around my dick, milking me as I began to thrust.

"Fuck, yes!" I grunted, pounding into her, my balls slapping against her ass. Emily's breasts jiggled with each thrust, and she cried out in Spanish, her words a mix of pleasure and encouragement.

"¡Más, Papi! Harder, please!"

I obliged, gripping her thick thighs, driving into her with abandon. Our bodies slapped together, creating a rhythm that had us both on the edge of ecstasy. I could feel my orgasm building, my balls tightening with the impending release.

"I'm gonna cum, baby," I warned, my voice strained.

"Cum inside me, Cameron," she panted, meeting my thrusts with her own. "Fill me with your hot load."

Her words sent me over the edge. I thrust one last time, burying myself deep within her, as my cock pulsated, shooting my hot cum into her welcoming pussy. Emily's pussy clenched around me, milking my shaft, as she climaxed with me, her walls rippling in pleasure.

We collapsed in a sweaty heap, our hearts racing and our bodies still trembling from the intense orgasms. I kissed her softly, tasting myself on her lips, as we lay there, content and satisfied.

"That was incredible, mi amor," Emily whispered, stroking my cheek. "I love how you fuck me."

I smiled, my heart full of love for this beautiful woman. "I love you, Emily. And I can't wait to make more unforgettable memories with you."

As we cuddled naked underneath a fur blanket, the fire crackling softly in the fireplace near us, I rubbed her belly thinking about our future child together.

"I love you. I can't wait to spend my life with you and our baby."

"Me, either Cameron. I love you so much. I know you are going to be a good dad."

"And you a mom. Thank you for giving me the family I've always wanted. I'm not alone now because of you."

"This is just the first one papi. There will be more to come."

"Oh, I know, I can't wait to have more kids with you."

Emily laughed. "I know you can't. I'm still dripping from the last time. I'm sure we won't have a problem having more kids."

"No, we won't. With a body like yours, I will always want more."

Emily laughed, "I love you papi."

"And I love you, Emily." We kissed once more before falling asleep in each other arms.

The next morning, we bid farewell to Scotland, our hearts heavy with the bittersweet feeling of leaving our honeymoon fantasy paradise. As we boarded the plane, I held Emily's hand, our fingers intertwined, and whispered, "Wherever we go, as long as we're together, it will always be home."

She smiled, her eyes filled with love and excitement for the future. "I can't wait to see what life has in store for us, my love. Together, we can conquer the world."

As the plane ascended into the sky, I knew that our journey was just beginning. Emily and I were ready to face the world as husband, wife and future parents, our love stronger than ever, and the possibilities were endless.

Don't miss out!

Visit the website below and you can sign up to receive emails whenever Michael Gordon publishes a new book. There's no charge and no obligation.

https://books2read.com/r/B-A-KEXRC-TJRLF

BOOKS 2 READ

Connecting independent readers to independent writers.

Did you love *The Geek's Dating Coach*? Then you should read *Will You Marry Me?*[1] by Michael Gordon!

[2]

The sun-kissed shores of Virginia Beach played host to a unique social experiment, a reality TV show that aimed to bring two strangers together in the hope of finding love. Among the eager participants were Zayden Moss, a charismatic former athlete, and Sabrina Chun, a reserved nurse with a rebellious streak. Their paths were about to collide in the most unexpected way, and the cameras were there to capture every moment. In the end of the experiment, will they stay married or be divorced? Find out in this season of Will you Marry Me?

1. https://books2read.com/u/4AlJdk
2. https://books2read.com/u/4AlJdk

Also by Michael Gordon

Will You Marry Me?
Love & War: The Battle of Virginia Beach
Forbidden Freedom
The Geek's Dating Coach

About the Author

Michael Gordon is a modern romance author who enjoys writing steamy, heart racing, interracial romances. When he's not writing, he's reading other swoon worthy interracial romance stories, traveling with his wife & kids, or watching sports.

www.ingramcontent.com/pod-product-compliance
Lightning Source LLC
LaVergne TN
LVHW041041150826
845672LV00001B/422

* 9 7 9 8 2 2 7 2 0 0 8 4 6 *